RETURNING FOR LOVE

A LONG VALLEY WESTERN ROMANCE NOVEL – BOOK 4

ERIN WRIGHT

WRIGHT'S ROMANCE READS

Copyright © 2017 by Erin Wright

ISBN: 978-1-979907-18-7

This book is a work of fiction. The names, characters, places and incidents are products of the writer's imagination or have been used fictitiously and are not to be constructed as real. Any resemblance to persons, living or dead, actual events, locales or organizations is entirely coincidental.

All rights reserved. No part of this book may be reproduced, scanned, or distributed in any manner whatsoever without written permission from the author except in the case of brief quotation embodied in critical articles and reviews.

To the Declans of the world:
*Finally, a story about you, and your very real struggles.
I hope I did you justice.*

And to Yvette Nolen:
*Thank you for sharing your story with me. I literally couldn't
have written this novel without you.*

CHAPTER 1

DECLAN

Late September, 2017

*D*ECLAN LOOKED AROUND the barn, surprised by how changed it looked. When a flock of women all descended on a place and put some real elbow grease into it…well, it could even make the Miller Family Farm barn look respectable.

To think that Stetson was hosting Wyatt's wedding at his place. *I don't know if Mom and Dad would believe this is happening and cry from happiness…or from shock.*

"Hey, Declan, can you help me?"

He turned to locate the source of his sister-in-law's voice. *Where is she?* Finally, he spotted her lugging in a box. In her matron-of-honor dress. He hurried over. "Jennifer, Abby will kill you if you get your dress dirty!" he scolded her, taking the box from her. She just shrugged.

"I'm the mother of the grandbaby," she said matter of factly. "I think Carmelita will defend me to the death."

Declan threw back his head and laughed. "True enough. Where are we going with the box?"

"Up to the front table. It's the last of the centerpieces that we're putting out. The guests will be here any minute now."

Music started twanging through speakers set up throughout the barn just for the occasion, and Declan got an itch to start line dancing to *Boot Scootin' Boogie*. But the clinking emanating from inside of the box reminded him that he was carrying a bunch of Mason jars around. Dropping and breaking them seemed like a sure-fire recipe for the wrath of his newest sister-in-law to come down on his head.

Newest sister-in-law. To think he had two of them now. He was the only single Miller brother left, something his brothers razzed him about endlessly, and his sisters-in-law spent their time trying to rectify. That blind date they'd set him up on last week…

His hands set out the jars, pre-filled with rocks from the creek, as his mind worked things over. As much as he liked seeing Jennifer and Abby happy, he had to put his foot down at some point. He'd only ever loved one woman and, well, she wasn't coming back to Sawyer any time soon. Maybe never. Which just meant that he'd better be happy as a bachelor, 'cause coupledom just wasn't for—

And then Jennifer was shoving a watering can with a long spout into his hands. "Guests are showing up; I need to go greet them. Finish filling these jars up to here," she pointed to the side of a jar, "with the water, and then put a candle in each one. I'll make sure someone comes along and lights the tea candles."

She was off before he could offer to light them himself. Oh well. He carefully filled each jar to the specified height with the watering can, then dropped the tea candles in.

They were real pretty, floating in the jars. When Abby had asked him if he thought she should do wildflowers or rocks with water and candles in the jars, he'd thought she was plumb crazy. Mason jars plus rocks plus tea candles plus water sounded like a disaster to him.

She hadn't been able to get the wildflowers in time, so rocks it was. And he had to admit, they looked real nice, shockingly enough.

The barn quickly filled up with people, a fresh layer of sawdust on the dirt floor and hay bales stacked in the corner adding to the effect. Jennifer had made Stetson drive every last tractor out of the barn to make room for the wedding, even the family relic — the first tractor ever owned by the Millers — and park them all out back, hidden out of sight. Stetson had argued for keeping the family relic around as an antique that everyone would love to look at but he'd been outvoted.

Declan rather wished the tractor was there. At least it was something he knew something about. He could stand around and talk to all the older farmers in the valley about it. That seemed a hell of a lot better than talking about Mason jars and rocks from creeks.

The music only got louder as more people filed in, or maybe it just seemed like they were turning it up louder. It was sure getting noisy though, either way. Carmelita saw him and came hurrying over, saying something he couldn't hear above the dull roar. He cupped his hand around his ear and bent down. She came up on her tippy-toes and shouted, "*Wyatt is looking for you!*"

Okay, maybe she didn't have to shout quite that loud right in his ear. He rubbed at it and nodded, looking around for the groom. Carmelita tugged on his arm again and he leaned down, warily this time. "*He is outside!*" she shouted.

He jerked away and nodded, heading for the door lickety-split. Anything to get out and breathe some fresh air.

DECLAN STOOD and tapped his knife against the side of his glass to get everyone's attention. He couldn't believe that he was in charge of starting off the rounds of toasts for Wyatt and Abby, but apparently, those were the duties of a best man. This was the second time he'd been a best man, but Stetson's wedding had been low-key compared to this one. Wyatt's idea of jetting off to Vegas had been quickly voted down by all of the women, and ever since, this wedding had taken on a life of its own.

Speaking of, he had about two hundred people all staring at him, waiting in hushed silence. He should probably talk or somethin'.

He was about to razz his older brother big time, but he figured if anyone in the world deserved it, it was Wyatt. He shot Wyatt a nervous grin before starting.

"Thank you so much for coming tonight to celebrate with Wyatt and Abby. I know most of you are here for the free food because you think Wyatt owes you something." The words were rushing out of his mouth while his nervous brain was praying that people would find the first joke funny. A comforting round of giggles and laughs answered his words.

He felt the tension begin to melt away and he looked around the barn, at all of the people smiling up at him. *Home.* No matter how much living in Sawyer sometimes drove him crazy, he also loved it.

"Many of you are well aware Wyatt is a bit difficult to deal with sometimes. What you may not know is that he used to be much worse." Declan waited, letting the people chuckle at his second joke. "I remember the time that Dad sent us out to get one of the wheat fields ready for planting. At the time, we had two tractors. One was older without a cab on it, and the other one was newer, with a cab, a radio, and air conditioning. All of the modern conveniences. Of course, Wyatt pulled rank, playing the older-brother card and claimed the new tractor for himself."

Declan looked over at Wyatt and winked. Wyatt's face was reddening; he knew which story was being told…and how it ended.

"The tractor had been sitting in the barn all winter and for most of the spring," Declan continued. "The new tractor was parked in front of the old one here in this barn, so I had to wait for Wyatt to get out of the way. I remember watching Wyatt climbing into the new tractor with the comfortable seat and the AC. I was so jealous.

"Wyatt made a big show of getting comfortable just to rub it in, settling back into the driver's seat with a happy sigh and stretch. He started the tractor, and then the sound of the rumbling engine was drowned out by Wyatt's screams as he flew out of the tractor. Apparently, a family of wasps had taken up residence in the AC vents over the winter, and when Wyatt started the machine, they got blown out of their home…and right into Wyatt's face."

The room erupted into gales of laughter and Declan joined in, looking at his brother, who was not laughing as hard as some of the guests, but he was laughing. Which just went to show how much Abby had changed him.

"I thought he was going to beat the tractor to

death with his hat as he tried to swat each and every wasp," Declan recounted as he turned to look directly at his brother. "If it makes you feel any better, I got stung a couple times too because I was laughing so hard, I couldn't run away."

Wyatt did let out a genuine laugh at that and Declan joined him. Declan allowed the room to enjoy the story before he continued.

"Abby has a maid of honor who I believe has some devilish stories to tell too, so I'll leave the embarrassing of the bride to Chloe, other than to say to Abby: I think your law enforcement training is about to come in very handy."

Declan let the chuckles die down, waiting until the audience took the cue that he was about to get serious. He'd razzed Wyatt enough for one day; it was time to be nice.

"Many of you also know that my brother has weathered some pretty serious storms of tragedy in his life. For many years, Wyatt held himself inside a very thick shell as a way to protect himself.

"Abby, somehow, you managed to break through that shell. Somehow, you're blessed with the right kind of love to speak to Wyatt in the way he needed most. Thank you for bringing our brother back." Declan raised his glass to the beautiful bride and the crowd joined him.

"Wyatt, Shelly and Sierra will never be replaced, but it is truly good to have you back. I just have one question for you: How does a guy like you get so lucky twice?" He inclined his glass toward his chuckling brother who was beaming at his new wife.

"To Abby and Wyatt: Best of luck, best of happiness, and best of love," Declan said, and took a sip of his champagne. His words were answered with a chorus of "Hear, hear," and with a grin, he sat down. His job was done, and he could relax.

Chloe stood up to give the maid of honor toast but as soon as she started talking, Declan's attention was caught by someone in the crowd. Someone who was looking straight at him.

Iris?

It couldn't be.

She couldn't be.

Last he'd heard, she was in Pocatello. Which was not here. But that color of red…he'd recognize it anywhere.

He turned towards Kathryn, one of Abby's bridesmaids and also the only one in the line-up who was currently unattached. Which was, by his reckoning, surely the reason he'd been paired up with her in the wedding lineup. This was Abby and Jennifer hard at work at playing matchmaker. He could've told them that Kathryn wasn't for him. She was too blonde. Too short. Too prone to bursts of staccato laughter. Too…not Iris.

"Hey, Kathryn," he said in a low voice. She turned from Chloe's speech and sent him a giant smile. He knew he was being inexcusably rude, talking during Chloe's turn in the spotlight, but he had to know.

"Yes?" she whispered back, leaning close. Her perfume, an overwhelming vanilla stench, made him want to gag. He leaned away a little. He couldn't breathe in too deeply or he'd end up in a coughing fit.

"Is that Iris McClain there in the back?" he asked, jerking his head towards the flame of red in the back of the room. How was it that he'd missed seeing it while he was giving his speech? It made him wonder if it was all an apparition. He had to know.

He had to know *now*.

"Yeah." The light in Kathryn's eyes dimmed. "Yup, she's back." Kathryn turned and pointedly started paying attention to Chloe's speech again, which as best as Declan could tell, was wrapping up. He turned and politely stared in Chloe's general direction as his knee bounced underneath the table impatiently. He couldn't focus on anything or anyone. *Talk faster, Chloe!*

Finally, the crowd began cheering and taking sips of their champagne, signaling the end of Chloe's speech, and so Declan obediently took a sip of his, feeling the alcohol go straight to his head. Or maybe something else was going straight to it.

Iris is here. In this barn. Right now.

He realized, belatedly, that his turn was up again…right about the time that Jennifer elbowed him in the ribs. He sent her a weak smile.

Whoops.

He stood up and said, "Dinner's done and the embarrassment of the happy couple is over, so if y'all can help us stack the tables against that wall," he pointed at the far wall, "and your dirty dishes over there," he pointed to a string of tables against another wall, "the dancing can begin!"

The DJ started up the music from the speakers and Declan took off like a shot as the shuffle of people around him began readying the barn for the dancing. Declan knew that Wyatt would want to string him up from the nearest tree for not helping out like he should be with the preparations...until he heard about Iris.

He'd understand then.

He came to a skittering stop in front of her, his heart in his throat. Or maybe it was just his bolo tie, cutting off all circulation.

"Iris?" he said softly, the world around him melting away. It *was* her. Brilliant red hair, longer than it was in high school, and the deepest, bluest eyes he'd ever seen.

Just like he remembered.

Her color was high in her cheeks as she looked up at him. "Hi, Declan," she said softly. Her eyes were drinking him in, and he was just sure she was as happy to see him as he was her.

Finally. The day he'd dreamed of, but never thought would come.

He held out his hands to her. "Let's hit the dance floor," he said. He wanted nothing more than to feel her in his arms again. Dancing was one of their favorite activities during high school, other than necking, of course.

She shook her head, biting on her lower lip, looking up at him with pain in her eyes.

"Don't you know?" she whispered softly.

CHAPTER 2

IRIS

*W*HY, WHY, WHY?

In a small town like Sawyer, gossip could travel faster than lightning, and cause a lot more damage. How was it that the one time – one time! – she wanted that gossip to happen, it hadn't? How was it that no one had bothered to tell Declan the truth about his ex-girlfriend?

She hadn't wanted to come tonight, of course. Who would want to attend the reception for their ex-boyfriend's brother and his new wife? Especially since she hadn't seen anyone in Sawyer for years, and certainly hadn't kept in touch with said ex-boyfriend *or* his brother?

But her mother being Betty Rae McLain, Iris was of course dragged there. When her mom didn't want to hear something, somehow, her hearing became strangely inconsistent, going in and out on a moment's notice. Considering she'd had this "hearing problem" since Iris was a small child, Iris was pretty sure it wasn't age related.

More like personality related.

Declan stared down at her, his deep brown eyes filled with concern. "What's going on?" he asked, his forehead creased. "Are you mar—"

"There you are!" Stetson's voice cut through their conversation as he clamped his hand down on Declan's arm. "I've been looking all over for you. Carmelita wants you hauling tables to get them out of the way. I've already backed the truck up outside the barn door." Stetson turned and spotted her. "Hey Iris," he said, flashing a dimpled grin. "I didn't know you were back in town." He tipped his hat to her and then her mother. "Mrs. McLain. Mr. McLain."

And then they were gone, disappearing into the crowd to go haul tables away.

Iris sunk further down into her seat, squeezing her eyes shut, wanting to die of mortification. She could hear her mother talking, but hell if she knew what she was saying. She could feel the heat of her blush set her face on fire, which no doubt meant her cheeks matched the color of her hair quite nicely.

Some days, I hate being a redhead…

She'd been doing so well. Forced as she was to attend, she'd strategically chosen a seat directly behind a rather…stout woman the next table over. As long as she kept Ms. Stout between her and the front of the barn, where Declan was doing his best man duties, she could eat the wedding feast, listen to

Declan as he told funny stories, and then hightail it out of there as soon as the real festivities started.

Because God knows, she wasn't gonna be much fun during that portion of the night.

Except, she'd cheated. She'd sat up after the fifth time that her mother had poked her in the ribcage, whispering that a true lady does not slouch, and took the opportunity to begin drinking her fill of Declan. If she was going to give up her refuge behind Ms. Stout, she might as well get something out of it.

Like study Declan's face, noting the changes and similarities from their years together in school. The way that the wrinkles crinkled around the corners of his eyes. How he'd become so much larger than the string-bean version she'd loved so many years ago. How she could detect just the barest glints of silver in his light brown hair under the lights of the barn.

He was even more handsome than she'd remembered. And that just wasn't fair at all.

He'd just finished ribbing his brother about hornets, sitting back down to let Chloe give her speech, when he'd caught her. She'd been staring right at him when his gaze swung and caught hers, their eyes irresistibly drawn to each other.

The way they'd always been around each other.

She couldn't pretend that she hadn't seen him, or stars above, that she hadn't been staring at him. They were way past such lies now, as much as she wished she could pretend otherwise.

Her plan, feeble as it might've been, had counted

on him knowing the truth, so she wouldn't have to tell him. Then he could stand on the other side of the room and pretend he didn't see her, and she could pretend she didn't see him.

You know, just like two 14-year-old teenagers would.

She rolled her eyes at herself. Even she could see the childishness of her plan. And anyway, obviously, Declan hadn't gotten the memo.

She looked over at her mom, who'd finally, blessedly gone silent. Her dad just looked at her quietly, pity in his eyes.

She hated pity.

With a passion.

"Can we go home now?" she asked, trying to keep the warble out of her voice. *Crying in the middle of Wyatt's wedding is simply not allowed, Iris Blue McLain, so don't even think about it.*

So she swallowed hard and pinned an overly bright smile on her face and pushed the tears away. They stood up, and leaning on her dad's arm, they made their way out of the barn and into the cool fall night.

She just had to wrap her head around the fact that she was happily heartbroken. Which was a strange state of affairs, sure, but true.

Someone else would do the dirty deed and tell him the truth, something someone should've done weeks ago, and so then she wouldn't have to. She was free to go back to her spinster life and she'd never have to see Declan again. She was plenty sure he wouldn't invite her to his wedding, and Stetson was already married, so she was hereby free from Miller weddings for the rest of eternity.

Which was good, because *never* was as soon as she wanted to attend another one.

Someday, when she could move out on her own again, she'd move far, far away from Sawyer so there wasn't even a chance of running into him down at the grocery store or on a street corner.

She'd move far away from the temptation that was Declan Miller.

CHAPTER 3

DECLAN

"WHAT THE HELL is going on with Iris McLain?" Declan hissed as soon as they neared the stacked pile of tables by the back door of the barn.

Stetson shot him a blank look. "What? Hell if I know. Listen, we need to hurry with these tables, because we still have decorating to do."

"Decorating?" Declan echoed, confused by the change in topics. Jennifer and Abby and Carmelita had done a bang-up job of decorating the barn; he didn't figure they needed any more help. Especially since they were three-quarters of the way through the reception. It seemed a little late to add more candles and rocks and glass jars at this point.

"Yes!" Stetson took a furtive glance around him and then leaned closer. "Wyatt's truck!" he whispered urgently.

Oh.

Of course.

As best man, it should've occurred to him. It hadn't, of course. Despite this being the second time that he'd held this honorary position, he really wasn't any better at it than he'd been the first time around. He needed about ten more brothers so he could get more practice in.

He groaned at the thought.

"What?" Stetson asked, as they slid a table into the back of Stet's truck.

"Oh, nothing. Just…daydreaming," Declan said, waving him off.

Ten more Wyatts? The world couldn't hold 'em. He loved his brother, especially since he'd recently removed his head from his ass, but not *ten* of him.

They finished loading the folding tables into the back of Stetson's truck and then grabbed decorating supplies out of the passenger seat. Stetson had come prepared.

The "decorating supplies" turned out to be empty soup cans tied together with orange yarn, Silly String in spray cans, and white sticks that looked like chalk but didn't feel a damn thing like them. Stetson caught his confused look. "Soap. It's used to write on vehicles but not cause damage."

Declan grunted his approval. Wrecking Wyatt's truck permanently…well, he wasn't entirely sure that even the joy of his wedding day would keep Wyatt from killing them both.

They got to work, tying the cans to the bumper

and writing well wishes all over the windows of the truck. Just as they were finishing up and ready to use the Silly String as the final touch, Jennifer came over. Twilight was deepening, but even in the shadows, she could tell what a grand job they'd done. He grinned at her, but she just scowled back.

"You guys!" she huffed. "Wyatt isn't going to like this." She was cradling Flint against her chest, a blanket wrapped over his tiny form to protect him against the chilly late September air. Winter was on its way.

Stetson just laughed. "I'm pretty sure that's the whole point," he said dryly. "If he liked it, that wouldn't make it nearly as fun of a prank."

She rolled her eyes at him but he just grinned back and pressed a kiss to her forehead. "Want the honors?" he asked, shaking the can and then holding it out to her.

She hesitated for a moment, and then snatched it out of his hand. "You, sir, are a bad influence!" she said as she began spraying the truck wildly. They were laughing and more Silly String was going everywhere, until finally, all of the cans were emptied.

Jennifer and Stetson leaned into each other, laughing so hard they had to hold each other up, Flint cradled between them, and Declan just looked at them, keeping the smile pasted on his face, but feeling a twist low in his gut. Would he *ever* get what his two brothers seemed to have found so effortlessly? Sure, Stetson almost had to lose his farm, and okay, fine,

Wyatt had had to spend months in jail, but the love between the couples was effortless.

It had only been that way once with Declan…and it couldn't happen again. He couldn't take that risk. He'd reacted instinctively when he saw Iris, running over to her like a lost puppy dog reuniting with its owner, thrilled and excited, but that couldn't happen again.

He wouldn't let it happen again.

His gut twisted harder.

"Who was that pretty redhead you were talking to earlier?" Jennifer asked, as if she could read his mind.

Scary, that.

"Iris McLain."

"Oh, that's the Iris I've been hearing about. Poor girl." Jennifer clucked her tongue and then began swaying, singing softly to Flint as she rocked.

"'Poor girl'? You know what happened?" Declan felt his stomach twist even tighter. He wasn't sure if he was going to throw up or pass out. Finally, someone who could tell him what the hell was going on.

Jennifer looked up, coming back to the moment. She'd obviously gotten wrapped up in her cooing.

"Oh. Yeah. She got in some terrible car wreck a month ago. Didn't anyone tell you?"

Declan staggered back, feeling all of the blood drain from his face.

An accident. Did she hit a deer on the road? Oh God, please don't let her have hit a deer.

"No," he whispered. Then, louder, "No. I didn't hear. Is she okay?"

Except, obviously she wasn't. She wouldn't have answered his question about dancing the way she had if she was perfectly all right.

Oh.

Oh.

She'd sat the whole way through the conversation, which Declan had found a little odd at the time, but had chalked up to her being nervous around him. But, maybe she couldn't stand up. Maybe, she was paralyzed from the waist down. Maybe, she was in a wheelchair and they'd just moved her to a folding chair so she wouldn't stand out from the crowd.

He wasn't sure he was breathing right. *Iris McLain, paralyzed?!*

Jennifer looked at him, concerned. "She's all right. Kinda. I hear her equilibrium is all messed up, though."

"Her equi…" His voice trailed off as he started to put the pieces together.

"Yeah, her balance. She falls over a lot now. Apparently, she has to walk with a cane everywhere she goes."

No wonder she didn't want to dance with me.

And there he was, running over to her, embarrassing her in front of her friends and family, asking her to dance when everyone else in the barn probably knew that she couldn't.

She likely wanted to smack him for making her look like an idiot in front of all the guests.

Except, she hadn't looked angry. She'd looked...heartbroken.

Stetson said, "Hey, we're going to go back inside and check on the happy couple!" in a tone that was way too enthusiastic in an obvious bid to give Declan some space, and then he was guiding Jennifer back inside, his arm around her shoulders as she cradled their baby to her chest. They were so happy together, such a great match. He never would've guessed that Stetson would be happy with a city girl, but there they went, disproving that theory.

And then the thoughts came rushing back – the thoughts that Declan had been suppressing. Iris, beautiful, independent, talented, athletic Iris, falling over. No balance at all.

How was that even possible? She'd been captain of the basketball team her junior and senior year. She was a natural. She could've gone on to play college ball but had decided to focus on her studies to become an RN instead, because she'd felt like that was more important. She could outrun, outshoot, outpass every other point guard who even tried to touch her. Seeing her on the court...

She had more talent than the rest of the team put together, but she never gloated. She always cheered her teammates on, and made them look good. Her younger sister, Ivy, had a hell of a time in high school, but Iris never did. She was so genuinely nice and thoughtful and caring, no one could find it in them to hate her.

And now she couldn't walk right?

He felt like the world had tilted off balance, like everyone had started walking sideways and he was left to try to navigate in this new world. How was it possible?

And what had he been thinking, running over to talk to her like that? He knew better. He didn't get to date people. Not anyone, not ever. It'd just been the surprise of seeing her – it'd thrown him for a loop. Caused him to forget everything he knew.

He shook it off. He couldn't just stand around and stare at the full moon, bathing the valley below in its flat, pale light. He'd go inside and find the happy couple and congratulate them and get them into their truck and swear he had no knowledge of how the truck got this way, and then send them off on their honeymoon. It was what a best man was supposed to do.

And Declan always did what he was supposed to do.

CHAPTER 4

IRIS

She stared down at the form in front of her, scrubbing wearily at her eyes with the palms of her hands. She was so exhausted. Why was it that paperwork drained her like this?

Well, at least in this case, she knew the answer to that. It was the legalese she had to read through – it was a killer. She wasn't sure if the lawyers themselves knew what these contracts meant. They probably just threw together a bunch of big words and figured no one would call them on their bullshit.

Which, they were right. At least in her case. Iris scribbled her name down at the bottom and then folded the papers and shoved them into the postage-paid envelopes.

She was about to become a medical coder.

After enrolling and graduating from the CNA program in high school, and then getting her nursing degree from Idaho State University, she had more medical knowledge in her little pinky than most people did in their whole bodies.

Now, Post Accident or PA as she liked to call it in her head, she may not be able to hover over people's bedsides and take their temperature, or recommend the best dosing schedule for a round of antibiotics, but she could code in medical records for insurance companies. It involved nothing *but* paperwork, Iris' least favorite part of being a nurse, but on the other hand, she could do it from home, it paid well, and it used her medical knowledge.

Oh, and she didn't have to stand while typing it all in. There weren't many jobs that offered all of those benefits. In fact, Iris was pretty sure there were exactly no other jobs that offered all of those benefits.

If there were, she'd probably do them instead, because medical coding…

Certainly not her dream job.

At least the Hermingston Medical College would allow her to test out of the vocabulary and human anatomy classes, so she wasn't going to be forced to spend months on end learning information she already knew backwards and forwards. All she had to do was learn the codes and the programs, and she'd be on her way.

Thankfully, learning had always come easy to her. That was how she and Declan had started spending time around each other to begin with, of course. He'd been getting his ass handed to him by Spanish 2, and although she wasn't a native-born speaker of Spanish, her grasp had been a lot stronger than his. She'd been hunkered down in the corner of the library one day, studying, when he'd come up to her and asked her if she offered tutoring for Spanish.

She'd known who he was, obviously. No teenage girl in a twenty-mile range had missed the Millers. Stetson was a lot younger than they were, so he hadn't been on her radar, but Wyatt always had that brooding bad boy persona and Declan...he was just nice. Thoughtful and nice and cheerful and funny and...drop-dead gorgeous.

Speaking of the Miller boys, Iris was thrilled to see Wyatt so happy with Abby, and God bless Abby for giving him his life back. After Sierra and Shelly died, a horrific accident her mom had told her about when she'd been living over on the other side of the state, Wyatt had become even more withdrawn. Even more prickly.

He was handsome – all the Miller brothers were – but he wasn't Declan. She didn't know how Abby could put up with Wyatt, actually, although the way he'd looked at her during their wedding last night... she'd never seen that man grinning as much as he had been during the festivities. Maybe Abby had finally busted down that wall that he'd always had around him.

Declan wasn't that way, though, not at all. Even as a teenager, he'd been incredibly thoughtful, and so much fun to be around. Studying Spanish with him, listening to his horrendous Spanish accent...she'd never laughed so hard in her life.

Oreo bumped her hand, letting out a small meow, and Iris jumped. She felt wetness on her cheeks and realized she'd been crying. Dammit all, she'd been crying over Declan Miller, for the 478th time.

"No more," she said to Oreo, who headbutted her hand, obviously not content with the pace of the pettings he was receiving. "Stetson or Wyatt or someone else has told him the truth about his ex-girlfriend; about how she's turned into a gimp. I'm never going to see him again, and I will be happy."

Oreo let out a yowl, and Iris laughed through the tears spilling down her cheeks. "Exactly," she said, with a nod for emphasis. "Now, let's go find you and Milk some food to eat." She pushed back from the table and grabbed her cane. Without her dad to hold on to like she'd had at the reception last night, she was dependent on her cane, even just when walking around her apartment. The very last thing she wanted to do was to reenact a 35-year-old version of the infamous, "I've fallen and I can't get up!" commercial.

She wouldn't let herself get to that point. Not ever. She'd had so much stripped from her; she wasn't going to have her independence stripped, too.

CHAPTER 5

DECLAN

*D*ECLAN RAN THE MASSIVE TRUCK over the bumps and furrows of the field, with only his seatbelt keeping him from taking a header through the front windshield. The wedding was over, the party was done, and now it was time to get back to work. Only a couple more weeks and harvest would be finished for the year.

He was thrown around as the truck hit a big dip and then back up again. He ground to a halt and threw the old beast into first gear and yanked on the parking brake. He hopped out and pulled on his work gloves. Time to get shit done.

But as he ran through the routine of harvest, he couldn't seem to keep his head in the game. All he wanted to do was wrestle with the question of Iris.

More specifically, what did he do about Iris.

His original plan had been, "Absolutely nothing at all." There was a reason that they weren't together.

Sure, the shock of seeing her had been overwhelming and he'd tried to ask her to dance, but now that moment had passed. He couldn't date Iris.

Except, after making himself into a jackass at Wyatt's wedding, he realized that he'd backed himself into a corner. If he didn't ask Iris out on a date, well now, he'd be sending the message loud and clear that he didn't want to date someone who wasn't whole and perfect. And that wasn't a message he wanted to send anyone, and certainly not the message he wanted to send Iris.

As near as he could figure it, he was now honor-bound to ask her out on a date. Just one, just to show that it wasn't her disabilities that were causing the problems. He had no idea what that date could involve, though. No hiking, no playing H.O.R.S.E. at the city park on the basketball courts, no dancing, no horseback riding…

They could go to a movie, he supposed, although that seemed awfully uninspired, and out to dinner, which seemed awfully unoriginal, and he'd have to make sure that the businesses they went to had no steps that needed navigating.

Then, once his ~~pity date~~ his duty was done, then he could go back to his life and she to hers and he wouldn't have to feel bad about making her feel bad. They could just drift apart and no one had to have any hurt feelings about disabilities or anything.

Except…

His hand paused on the bed of the truck as he

was pulling the tarp down into place. What if she was dating someone? Hell, she could even be married for all he knew.

Jennifer hadn't mentioned a boyfriend, a fiancé, or a husband for that matter, but that didn't mean a damn thing. She probably didn't know their history and didn't know why Declan had been asking all of those questions. Iris could have some boyfriend tucked away, back in Pocatello or Boise or in Los Angeles for hell's sakes.

Maybe that's why she'd said, "Don't you know?" It was awfully presumptuous of him to assume she was single.

He grunted as he got back into the beast and started the engine, the rumble vibrating through the driver's seat as he threw it into first gear. He didn't like the idea of Iris having a boyfriend because he probably wasn't good enough for her. Nobody was good enough for her.

That was all.

He wasn't jealous, of course. He had no reason to be jealous. He and Iris hadn't been exclusive for years. Thirteen, to be exact. Not that he was counting.

The idea that she would be single was downright ludicrous, really, unless the whole state of Idaho was filled with blind and stupid men.

Still, he ought to ask Jennifer to find out. Just in case. If Iris was seeing someone, well, his duty was done. He could move on. And if she was single, he'd

~~ask her out on one pity date~~ do his duty, and *then* he could move on.

Either way, he and Iris McLain weren't meant to be. He'd figured that out a long time ago, and no amount of gorgeous red hair could change that fact.

CHAPTER 6

IRIS

Gripping her cane with one hand, she held tightly to the handle of the grocery sack with the other as she listened to her sister chatter in her ear through her Bluetooth earpiece.

"Listen," Iris said as soon as she sensed a break in the conversation, "we need to talk about Mom and Dad's 40th wedding anniversary party." She was making her way down the two steps to the front door of the mother-in-law apartment and then through to her kitchen. This was her sixth load of groceries into the house; everything was slower when she had to "waste" one hand holding on to a cane and thus could only carry groceries with the other hand. She dropped the bag on the counter and then trudged back toward the open door.

She was letting cool air in by leaving the door propped open, but she couldn't find it in herself to give a damn. Managing a cane, a bag of groceries, *and* the door knob? That was a recipe for disaster if she ever heard one. She'd just have to throw on a sweater, once she'd managed to get everything inside.

"Ugh," Ivy groaned dramatically. "Iris, I do not want to go back to Long Valley."

"I know, but this is Mom and Dad's big four-oh. You have to come back home for it. I bet you Tiffany and Ezzy aren't even here in the valley anymore."

"You just moved back yourself. Are you sure?"

"No," Iris admitted with a small laugh. "You're right, I'm not sure. But I am sure that we can skip sending them an invitation, so for the week or so that you're here, you can hide out, away from them. If I have to live in Mom and Dad's mother-in-law apartment for the foreseeable future, you can at least come stay with me for a week. It's only fair. I'll let you sleep on the couch."

Iris'd made it back to the car and was eyeing the last item dubiously. She'd known even when she'd bought it that it was going to be damn awful trying to get it into the house. But grocery stores didn't sell cat food by the cupful.

She sat down on the tailgate of her car for a moment, catching her breath. She'd never realized it was such an athletic adventure just hauling in groceries.

"Hmph. Well, speaking of old news," Ivy said in an obvious bid to change topics, "have you run into Declan yet?"

"Ugh. Yes…?"

"Why did that sound like a question instead of an answer?" Ivy asked, laughing. "Either you've run into him or you haven't."

"Well, we only spoke for a few moments, and then Stetson needed his help. He...he asked me to dance."

Iris hated that her voice broke just then. Hated it with a passion. It'd been a little over a month now since the night of her wreck. She shouldn't be upset any longer. Crappy things happened to good people all the time.

Her lot in life was just a bit crappier than most, was all.

"Oh." Ivy just went quiet because really, what else was there to say?

But Iris couldn't leave it alone. Finally, someone to talk to who wasn't her mother, pushing her to "just get back out there."

"Somehow, the gossip chain here in Long Valley failed to pass the word on to him that his ex-girlfriend is now practically a cripple, and sure as hell can't dance. You know, this is the same gossip chain that had Mom knowing that I'd snuck out of the house before I'd barely got my foot over the lip of the bedroom window. I don't think I sneezed in high school without someone somewhere telling someone else about it. And yet, the one time that I wanted the knowledge to pass on, the gossips of the world went mum."

"Iris, you are not a cripple. You are beautiful and smart and amazing and it just so happens that you fall sideways unexpectedly. And run over things that are right in front of you."

Iris laughed at that. Painfully true, in every sense of the word.

"But the doctor said you'll get better over time," Ivy plowed on. "You just need to give yourself some space and forgive yourself for not being the Sawyer High School basketball star anymore."

"Yeah, my days of dribbling up and down the court are long gone." It seemed like so long ago that she'd been able to dribble circles around her opponents, putting the ball up and taking the shot to win a game. It was a glorious, freeing, amazing feeling.

That she'd never, ever feel again.

"Well, be that as it may, you don't want to go on a date with Declan Miller anyway. He's the one who chose farming over you, for God's sake. He's an ass. Plus, you don't want to be stuck in podunk Idaho for the rest of your life. As soon as you're healed up, you should move down here with me. The weather is so much better in California, I promise. No snow, no horrific winds, and not a pine tree in sight."

"I like pine trees!" Iris said with a laugh. She pushed off the bumper of the car and turned around, eyeballing the sack of cat food again. It was time to get the thing inside since it certainly wasn't going to get there by itself.

Well, technically, she could wait until her father got home and he could carry it in for her – she was rather sure that was the whole idea behind them forcibly moving her into the MIL apartment — but she was sick of everyone doing everything for her. She wanted to unload groceries all by herself — was that so much to ask?

"You like pine trees? Well, everyone is entitled to be wrong," Ivy said, laughing, and Iris just rolled her eyes, even though her younger sister couldn't see her. When her high school graduation had rolled around, Ivy's bags had been packed. She walked across the stage, accepted her diploma, and kept on going. She didn't even stay for the graduation party that night. She was leaving Sawyer, Idaho, and she was never coming back.

It was no surprise that she wouldn't think a farmer was worth dating. Iris would've worried that Ivy'd had a personality transplant if she'd tried to argue otherwise.

"Whether or not I *should* date Declan," Iris said, "I *won't* date Declan. Mostly because I won't be seeing him again." It'd been five days since the wedding, and she hadn't seen hide nor hair of the man. Just like she'd expected, someone had finally told him the truth.

Which she was just fine with. Happy about, even.

Very happy.

It would've been nice to finally get some answers, and according to her friends, it was a lack of those answers that were keeping her from moving on. But she'd lived this long without them; she didn't need them before and she didn't need them now.

She was about halfway back to the apartment when the bag started to slip out from under her arm. She swung her other arm around wildly, trying to catch it before it went tumbling to the ground, but they all went tumbling instead. She landed with a heavy thud on top of the bag, busting the top seam open and sending cat food everywhere.

"Are you okay?" Ivy yelled in her ear, obviously hearing the ruckus. Iris rolled off the bag and stared up at the brilliant blue sky.

"Yeah, just fine," she said with a shaky half-laugh. "Apparently, I am no longer friends with cat food bags."

"What?" Ivy asked, confused.

"Never mind. Listen, I gotta go. We'll talk later this week – we need to get some planning done on this party. It'll be here before we know it."

"Yeah, yeah, okay. Are you sure you're all right?"

Iris pushed herself to her feet, surveying the damage in front of her. Cat food had gone everywhere, and there was now a busted seam that she would need to be careful not to spill more food out of.

But, in good news, the bag was now much lighter since half of it was on the ground.

There was a silver lining to everything, it turned out.

"Yeah, I'm fine. Love ya, sis. Talk to you later."

She pressed on the bluetooth ear piece to turn it off and then swung back towards the MIL apartment. She'd need to get a bucket or bowl to pick up the spilled cat food. Time to clean up yet another one of her messes.

CHAPTER 7

DECLAN

He knocked on the door and then stepped back, clutching his bouquet of late-blooming irises to his chest. With a name like Iris, she'd either love the flower or hate it, but luckily, Declan knew which one from their high school days. Also luckily, Carla at Happy Petals was able to get in a bouquet for him. He hated to think how far she'd had to go to find irises at this time of the year.

Iris opened the door, looking out quizzically and then her mouth dropped open in surprise.

"Declan!" she exclaimed. He could tell she would've expected a grizzly bear before she would've guessed he'd show up, and considering it'd been six days since they'd seen each other at the wedding, he couldn't blame her. It'd taken him time to figure out what to do for their date, and to get irises ordered in. If he was going to talk her into this, he needed something to help sweeten the pot.

Oh, and he also had to find the time to ask Jennifer if Iris had someone special in her life. He didn't like to focus on the joy he'd felt at the news that Iris was single. That was just…heartburn.

Pleasant heartburn.

He thrust the irises at her. "Royal purple, your favorite," he said with a nervous smile. He was trying to hide that nervousness, but was pretty sure he was failing.

Miserably.

She stepped back and held the door open, taking the irises from his hands as he walked past into the apartment. "I love them," she said, burying her face in the irises for a moment. She navigated her cane, the irises, and the closing of the front door with ease, which he was happy to see. Maybe stories of her clumsiness were overblown.

Then again, she was 35 years old and walking with a cane. Maybe she was just good at hiding her disabilities.

"Carla at Happy Petals got them in for me. I'm glad you like them. I came over to find out if you were free to go with me to Franklin this Friday." It came out in a rush but she seemed to understand it anyway because she just froze for a moment, staring at him.

"Franklin? Are you…sure?" she breathed.

"I wouldn't have come over to ask if I wasn't," he said with a teasing grin. "I thought it'd be fun to attend the music festival and eat all of the fair food that's totally awful for you, and catch up on old times. Find out what you've been up to lately."

She froze and he froze, and time just stopped.

He gulped. Hard. "I mean, *other* than…that," he said, gesturing at the cane in her hand.

She glared at him for a moment longer and then nodded. Once. "What time are you going to come pick me up?" she asked, ignoring his faux pas for the moment. *Thank God.*

"Around two?" he asked.

"Sure, that works."

"Okay, good." He backed towards the door slowly. "Good talk. See you later," and then he was escaping outside and into the autumn air. He closed the door behind him and groaned. Hopefully between now and then, he'd learn how to talk to Iris again. They used to be able to talk for hours without missing a beat. She'd been not only his girlfriend, but his best friend, there for a while.

And now, all he seemed to be able to do was jam his cowboy boot into his mouth whenever he got around her.

Not exactly the start to their date that he'd been wanting.

He crunched his way through orange and brown leaves skittering across the yard, and berated himself. Actually, this was exactly the start to their date that he'd been wanting. This was a pity date, nothing more. If it went awkwardly, all the better. Then she wouldn't be surprised when he didn't ask her out again.

Because he wasn't going to ask her out again. That wasn't part of the plan. One and done.

Nothing more.

CHAPTER 8

IRIS

*I*RIS PACED THE LIVING ROOM of her apartment, waiting for Declan to pick her up.

Or rather, she wanted to pace the living room.

In reality, she was simply sitting on her couch, too afraid she'd run into something or fall over and hurt herself before Declan even arrived. Wouldn't that just be a fine start to the afternoon – a faceplant into the carpet. He could walk into her house and find her sprawled out on the floor, her dress up around her head.

No siree bob. She was going to keep her butt planted on the couch until he showed up. She could just pace in her mind.

Unfortunately, pacing in her mind didn't work nearly as well as she would've liked, because none of her nervous energy was being worn off. She looked at the silver watch bracelet on her wrist and groaned.

Only three minutes since the last time she'd looked at her watch, and ten minutes before Declan was supposed to show. He was a punctual person so the chances were pretty good that he'd actually be there in ten minutes, but even so, right then? Ten minutes might as well have been a thousand years.

Her stomach was twisting in so many knots, worried about how this date was going to go and all of the myriad of ways she could screw it up, she was pretty sure the first thing she was going to do to screw it up was throw up all over Declan's cowboy boots.

Wouldn't that be a fine way to start the date. She almost preferred the dress-up-around-her-ears outcome.

She reminded herself that she was going to use this date to pin him to the wall, like a botanist pins a butterfly to a board. She was going to get answers, dammit. Years of no answers was about to come to an end.

Milk jumped up onto the couch and snuggled up against her thighs, looking up at her with piercing green eyes as she tried her Jedi mind trick to convince Iris to pet her.

"You know you don't have to use your Jedi skills on me," Iris said with a laugh, stroking her beautiful brown tabby body from head to rump. "I'll pet you whether or not you stare at me intently." Milk's purrs just grew louder and she stretched out on Iris' lap, really getting into the pettings now. "You know, it's a good thing I love you, or I wouldn't put up with you shedding your hair all over my clothes just before I go out on my big date." Milk flicked her tail, completely unconcerned about the summer fur she was shedding everywhere in preparation for her winter coat.

Iris let the long strokes and the rumble and purrs soothe her. She felt a little less anxious already. This was just Declan. There was nothing between them. That'd died years ago, when he'd chosen farming over her, as her sister so eloquently put it. This wasn't a real date. They would just go out this one time, catch up on old times, she'd get her answers, and then they'd never see each other again.

Ugh. But this was Declan.

The one guy she'd never been able to get over, no matter how many guys had asked her out while she was at Idaho State University. Back when she'd been in shape, back when she'd been confident on her feet and sure about where she was going and who she was, she could have had a date every Friday night if she'd wanted.

She'd found, though, that the guys who asked her out were too tall or too short; too loud or too quiet; trying too hard, or not trying at all.

Too…not Declan.

Her roommate, Rebecca, had told her that she wasn't over Declan, but Iris had ignored her, mainly because it didn't matter. Whether she was "over" him or not, she wasn't going to be dating him anymore, so why think about it?

Except thinking about Declan was all she did

while at ISU and then afterwards, when she got the job at Portneuf Medical Center.

A knock on the front door startled her out of her thoughts, and when she jumped, Milk took off like a bolt for the bedroom.

Fine. I can face Declan all by myself. I'm a big girl.

She heaved herself to her feet and grabbed her favorite walking stick, a piece of hand-carved polished hickory wood. Her parents had bought it for her when they brought her home from the hospital, and she just loved it. It was bad enough that she had to have assistance while walking; she didn't want to have to walk with an orthopedic cane. The black canes with four little feet sprouting out of the bottom? Those were for the birds. Or people over the age of 85.

She got to the front door and pulled it open to reveal Declan, bearing…

"Ohhh!" she squealed happily when she spotted the chocolate cheesecake in his hands. Her favorite. "Where did you get it?" She went to take it from him but realized that balancing the large cheesecake and her walking stick all at the same time would be tough. Declan seemed to understand her hesitancy and just carried it inside for her, and over to the kitchen counter.

"The Muffin Man. Have you been there yet since you got home?"

"No, but I heard that the Dyer's grandson recently took over when they retired. I also heard that he's—"

She stopped herself just in the nick of time. She was not going to discuss how cute the new baker was with Declan of all people.

"As cute as his food is delicious?" Declan finished with a twinkle in his eye.

"It's possible I heard something like that," Iris said primly, as if she hadn't heard how drool-worthy Gage Dyer was from about 15 women down at the grocery store. Sure, they could all stand around and talk about the baker being cute, but they couldn't be bothered to tell Declan that his ex was a cripple?

There were days she didn't understand this town. About 365 of them a year.

"You ready?" he said with a gallant smile as he held his arm out for her. She slipped her arm through his and with the help of her walking stick, made it out the door and up the two steps to the driveway, and into the warm autumn afternoon. It was fall in the Goldfork Mountains, which meant that it could be 9 or 90 degrees on any given day. Today, the weather was blessedly warm, which she was sure the music festival coordinators appreciated.

They made it over to Declan's truck, bigger and newer than the beat-up beast he'd driven in high school. She bit her lip as she looked at the passenger side door. Even with a step up, the front seat just seemed so damn far up there. She took a deep breath for courage and scrambled up and in, swallowing her cry of joy that she hadn't fallen on her head in the process. Declan didn't notice her hesitation, which she counted as a win. Every time she could hide her fears or her worries or her disabilities from others, she'd won a small victory.

She would take all the small victories she could get.

"Is it Old Time Fiddlers again this year?" she asked as soon as Declan had made it around to the driver's side and had settled in. The diesel engine roared to life, and Declan let it settle down before he answered.

"Yup. And a couple of local acts that are starting to make it regionally. I think they're trying to raise funds to travel to Nashville."

Someone who is chasing their dreams. Who can chase their dreams. Iris bit back her envy and reminded herself that she'd had her chance, too. Hers was just cut a little short, was all.

She should ask him right now, and just get it over with. But as she turned to study his profile as he drove, she realized that she didn't want to ruin their date this early in. She'd wait until the end of the date, and then ask him. No reason to make the whole afternoon awful, right?

She absolutely, positively was not ignoring a huge problem that needed to be dealt with. She was simply…postponing the discussion.

There was a big difference.

They fell into an easy chit-chat as they made the 30-minute drive to Franklin, laughing about pranks they'd pulled on their hated high school English teacher. There were only two English teachers at Sawyer High School. One was beloved by all, and one was…not.

Somehow, they'd both been stuck with the "not" all four years.

"At some point, you have to wonder if our parents were paying the administration to stick us in with her, because they thought we needed to learn a lesson or something from it – that it 'builds character,'" Iris said, laughing. "I mean, what are the chances that we'd get her all four years?"

Declan looked over and grinned. "Or maybe our parents weren't paying a bribe to the superintendent, and the other parents were! Remember all of those ditto sheets she made us do?"

"High school English, and we were filling out multiple-choice quizzes and coloring in puzzles to reveal a hidden picture. Who ever thought that they'd hide a drawing of Shakespeare in one of those puzzles?"

Declan shook his head, smiling slightly. "I don't think any teacher in the history of teachers deserved to retire more than her. I didn't learn a damn thing about English from her class, except to hate English." A small grimace crossed his face and then quickly passed, his smile firmly back in place. Iris wondered for a moment if she'd actually seen what she thought she had, or if it was just a trick of her mind.

"It's amazing she hung in there until she hit her 60s, isn't it?" she said after a moment. "I was afraid she'd be one of those teachers who was still around in her 80s, but I think the principal took her aside and heavily encouraged her to retire. I kinda wonder if she isn't the reason that I fell in love with science and the medical world like I did. At least in biology, no one made me color Shakespeare's head."

"Biology…" Declan repeated with a half-grimace, half-grin.

"Yeah! Okay, mister, it's been years. You can tell me the truth now. Did you or did you not release all of those frogs into Mrs. Westingsmith's room?" she demanded, crossing her arms and glaring at him.

He suddenly became very interested in the road ahead. They were almost to Franklin and traffic from the music festival was clogging the highway. They slowed to a crawl.

"Ummmm…uhhh…" he stuttered. "I…uhh…"

"You did!" she crowed. "I knew it! Your innocent face isn't so innocent. Every time you plaster that 'I'm an angel' look on your face, I'm damn sure you've been the devil instead! You have everyone else fooled, but not me."

"Well, not my dad either." He grimaced. "I never thought I'd walk again after he heard about the frog incident. He paddled my ass good that night."

"Hey, I liked Mrs. Westingsmith! If you were going to unleash a ton of frogs into someone's room, why not our English teacher?"

"Because I didn't have a test in her class."

Iris let out a howl of laughter. "How on earth did

you graduate from high school?" she asked, wiping her tears away.

"No clue," Declan said cheerfully. "Actually, I think the principal wanted me out of his hair. He started calling me Moses."

"Moses?" Somehow, Iris had missed this. Or she'd forgotten in the ensuing years.

"Yeah, for bringing a plague of frogs down upon the school. I don't think he let Mrs. Westingsmith keep that many frogs in the terrarium after that. I heard through the grapevine that he told her it was too much temptation to high schoolers. He mighta been right about that."

She shook her head in mock disapproval. "The next time someone tries to tell me all about how sweet and kind you are, I'm gonna tell them about the Moses story," she warned him.

He threw her a triumphant look. "Eh, no one will ever believe you. I've got this whole town fooled."

She let out another round of laughter. "Oh heavens, I should secretly tape you and show it to all the little old ladies in town. Otherwise, they'll think I'm lying."

He waggled his eyebrows at her. "I just have to bat my eyes at them and they'll forgive me for anything."

She rolled her eyes, smiling. "You know, you're probably right." He had more charm in his little toe than ten other guys did combined together.

Something he was well aware of.

They pulled into a large gravel parking lot, and

after he came around and helped her down, they began to move their way across it, towards the discordant sound of musical instruments warming up. Declan had slung a jean quilt over his shoulder, which she assumed was for them to sit on. Always thoughtful; that was Declan.

And strong. Holy cow, she'd forgotten how muscular he was. Or maybe, he'd bulked up since high school. She didn't remember this many muscles rippling under his skin back then. He'd started to gain muscle their first two years in college together, but nothing like this. She wondered if he bench-pressed combines every morning before breakfast.

She snuck a glance up at him through her eyelashes to check to see if he was embarrassed to be out with a cripple. Did he care that she was using a walking stick, and he had to hold on to her other arm? He didn't seem to be; he was looking around, tipping his hat as they went past women, smiling at everyone. He must've sensed her looking at him because he glanced down at her and grinned.

She blushed.

Dammit, I always get caught when I sneak peeks. You, Iris, are no Nancy Drew.

They found a small tree casting a little shade and he spread out the blanket for her to sit on. He helped her lower down to the ground and tuck her legs up underneath her, and then after a promise to be right back, he took off for the food trucks. She watched him in action; tipping his hat, smiling, picking up a dropped dollar bill and handing it back to the little girl who'd lost it...

She wondered for a moment if Mrs. Miller was looking down at her middle son and seeing what an amazing man he'd grown up to be. She sure hoped so; she was sure Mrs. Miller would be proud of how he'd turned out. Iris had been dating Declan for a little over four years when she'd died. Car wreck. Declan changed after that, and it wasn't much longer after that before he suddenly decided that farming was more important than her.

Something I'm going to pin him down about tonight.

She debated asking him when he came back with their food, before the Old Time Fiddlers really got started, but decided to wait until after the concert. She could ask him on the way home. That way, they could talk privately, without worrying about anyone overhearing them. Plus, then she wasn't ruining the concert.

That was the smart thing to do. Totally not cowardly at all.

He made his way back bearing all of the junk food she absolutely should not be eating...yet absolutely adored. He had an elephant's ear in one hand and two turkey legs in another, along with a giant Icee.

She grinned up at him when he paused at the edge of their blanket. "Want some help with that?" she asked eagerly, holding her hands up for the elephant ear. He passed it down to her with a teasing wink, and then settled onto the blanket next to her. She pulled off a piece of the warm, fried bread, thick with cinnamon and sugar on top, and popped it into her mouth, chewing ecstatically.

He watched her, his eyes growing dark as he smiled at her. "I can see you love fry bread as much as you did in high school," he said with a laugh tinged with…lust?

Surely not. She walked with a cane and tripped over the smallest things. Sometimes, she wondered if she was tripping over air molecules. She wasn't someone who would inspire lust, especially not in a man like Declan Miller. He was just…

Huh.

She wasn't quite sure what he was staring like that for, actually. She sent him a quizzical smile and his face instantly brightened, and whatever that was, was gone.

Thankfully, the warming up of the fiddles came to a sudden end, and an older woman was getting up on the small platform to face the waiting audience. She thanked them all for coming, and then started the group off with a flourish.

As the group began to play classics mixed in with newer tunes, the audience began clapping along, whooping and hollering. After one particularly impressive solo in *The Devil Went Down to Georgia*, the whole audience was yelling and screaming like they were at a rock concert. Iris turned to Declan and they grinned at each other, the excitement and fun almost palpable in the air.

Why is Declan here with me?

The thought came out of nowhere, and Iris paused, the music and the crowd around her fading away.

I'm not the woman he fell in love with so many years ago. Why did he ask me out? Why are we here?

She had no answer, and that scared her more than anything.

CHAPTER 9

DECLAN

HE BAND FINISHED The Devil Went Down to Georgia *and the crowd went wild. Declan whooped and hollered along with the best of them, and turned to smile at Iris. That was one of her favorite songs in high school. She must be…*

Off in her own little world?

She was staring off into the distance in some sort of trance, not paying the least bit of attention to anyone or anything around her.

"Are you okay?" he asked her and she jumped slightly, turning to him with a huge smile on her face that didn't reach her eyes.

"Oh, absolutely," she said over the din. "Isn't this concert great?"

"It is." But before he could say anything more, the Old Time Fiddlers started into *Oh! Susanna* and the crowd was clapping along again, singing the lyrics at the top of their lungs. This time, Iris' smile did reach her eyes as she began clapping and bellowing too. He couldn't help grinning back, and decided to push down his worry. Whatever it was that she'd been thinking about, she'd moved on.

Like he should be doing. He'd forgotten how much fun it was to be around Iris. They'd spent the last two years of high school and the first two years of college together – they'd pretty much gotten along like two peas in a pod. She was friendly and kind and thoughtful, and he found that he could relax and just be himself around her, not something he could say about everyone, and certainly not what he could say about the blind dates that Abby and Jennifer had set him up on in the last month.

Didn't they realize that he couldn't date someone?

Not even Iris.

Especially not Iris.

The Old Time Fiddlers swapped out for a local act, The Boot Stompers, and the hours faded away. By the time the music ended, their pile of fair food had been demolished, leaving only a burnt corner of the fry bread and some watery syrup at the bottom of the Icee cup. Declan threw their trash away and then helped Iris to her feet.

The crowd surged around them, all stampeding toward the parking lot, but Declan realized that he wasn't in any hurry. Normally, he was one of those men standing towards the back of the crowd, close to the exit, ready to bolt as soon as an event was done, so he could hightail it out before the masses descended upon the parking lot.

But with Iris on his arm, life was suddenly a lot slower.

And strangely, he didn't seem to mind one bit. He rather enjoyed how she was hugging his arm, snuggling it up against her. He'd always loved helping others, but once Stetson found Jennifer and Wyatt fell in love with Abby, he'd been at loose ends. His brothers didn't need him like they had before. He was happy for them, of course, truly happy, but being able to take care of someone again warmed up a part of him he hadn't even realized was unhappy.

He snuck a sideways glance at Iris as they strolled through the grass. She was the same as ever, and yet, indefinably different. A few more wrinkles around her eyes, longer red hair…she was a woman now, not a girl.

He'd thought since the first moment he'd laid eyes on her back in junior high – when he first started looking at girls that way, instead of as annoying humans who squealed and cried a lot – that she was quite possibly the most beautiful girl he'd ever seen. It'd taken him until their sophomore year to ask her to tutor him; until their junior year to ask her out on a date.

Never once did he change his mind on the topic of her beauty – not then, not now. When he'd switched colleges halfway through his bachelor's degree and had moved up to northern Idaho, he'd tried to forget her. He'd asked out every blonde and brunette he could find.

None of them were Iris McLain.

The crowds were almost gone by the time they got to his truck. He helped her inside and then hurried around to his side. They headed back towards Sawyer, Garth Brooks singing about thunder as they cut along through the gathering darkness. It'd been a damn amazing day and Declan admitted to himself that he didn't want it to end. This was supposed to be a one-and-done. A pity date. It'd turned into…

Well, not that.

"I—" they both said at the same time, and then started laughing.

"You go first," Declan said.

"No, it's okay. What were you going to say?" Iris responded.

"Just that…" He blew out a breath as he drove, thinking about how he wanted to say this. "I had so much fun tonight, Iris, I really did. Next weekend, what would you think about going to Copperton with me? They've fixed the washed-out bridge and the old steam engine is running again. We could take a train ride and eat dinner. You've been gone to Pocatello for so long, you might've forgotten what it's like over here in western Idaho. A train ride through the scenery might be a lot of fun."

Anything was fun around Iris, but a train ride seemed especially fun. It was a damn creative idea if he did say so himself.

She turned and studied him in the lights of the dashboard for a moment. And then another moment. The silence got longer and he started to second-guess himself. Maybe Iris hadn't felt that same spark he had. Maybe she didn't want to be around him. Maybe she—

"I'd enjoy that," she said softly.

Oh.

Good.

He was surprised at the strength of the happiness that rushed over him at her words. Her saying yes meant a lot to him.

Probably a lot more than it should.

He pushed that thought away.

"Great!" He shot her a grin and she returned it. He turned up the radio and they began bellowing out *She Thinks My Tractor's Sexy!* all the way home.

CHAPTER 10

IRIS

*I*RIS RUBBED AT HER EYES. They felt like #10 sandpaper was lining them. Memorizing medical codes was about as much fun as she'd thought it would be.

Which was to say, absolutely no fun at all.

Oreo was busy giving Milk a bath in her ear, loudly and persistently. "You two are so noisy," she groaned. Oreo paused for a moment, looking at her inquisitively, and then began the bathing again. Milk just ignored her completely.

She looked down at her jeans and pearl-snap button shirt. After wearing a skirt to the music festival last week, she'd realized that life was already hard enough. She didn't need to have "Management of skirt" on the list, too. Wranglers wouldn't blow up around her head, no matter how hard the wind was blowing.

And boy was it blowing today. Last week's

beautiful fall weather had turned last night, and today, it was nothing but browns and golds when she looked out the window. The trees were losing their leaves, and fast. She figured that just meant that the train ride would be even more beautiful.

The train ride. She really needed to confront Declan today. She'd been so set to do it last week, had even started to ask, when he'd been sweet and asked her out on another date. She'd known she should say no. She'd known that she should instead demand answers. But instead, out came a "yes."

She'd spent the week psyching herself up for this afternoon. She could do it. She would do it. She had to do it.

Whether or not she wanted to do it.

This time, when Declan knocked, she wasn't as jumpy. She shut the lid to her laptop, grateful that she could stop pretending that she was studying, and pushed herself to her feet. She grabbed her fancy cane – rosewood with a garnet inset – and made her way to the door. She opened it to find…

"Declan!" she exclaimed, half laughing, half scolding. "You can't keep bringing me presents every time you come over." She was eagerly holding her hands out for his puzzle, though, the laughter greatly outweighing her scolding. She couldn't help feeling incredibly special that he remembered her so well.

"It's cats. I figured you'd love that." He looked past her and towards the couch, where Oreo and Milk had paused in their bathing and were watching them with great interest. "Speaking of, it looks like you've got cats already. What are their names?"

She tucked the adorable 500-piece puzzle under her arm and followed him towards the cats snuggled up. "Milk and Oreo," she said proudly. She put the box down on the coffee table so she could snuggle them. "This is Oreo," she said, picking him up.

"Hmmm…I get the Oreo name, considering the black-and-white fur," Declan said, taking him and snuggling him up against his chest. *Damn, cats look good on him.*

Everything looks good on him.

"But how did you pick the name Milk for that one?" he said, gesturing towards the brown tabby on the couch. "Unless that's milk that's gone bad…"

She laughed and rolled her eyes. "No. I got Oreo first, and when I went to pick out a second cat, I had every intention of choosing a white one so I could name her 'Milk.' But, I fell in love with her instead." She stroked Milk's head and Milk began purring loudly, closing her eyes in bliss. "She has such a loving personality, I just couldn't walk away from her. So, I decided to stick with the name 'Milk' anyway."

Declan set Oreo back down on the couch, and he streaked off towards the bedroom. "Rotten milk," she muttered under her breath, intentionally loud enough for Declan to hear. "That's my baby you're talking about there."

"Hey, you're the one who named a brown cat 'Milk.' You should've named her 'Chocolate Milk.'"

"Too long. I wanted to really be able to holler her name when she was being a shithead."

He let out a belly laugh as they meandered out into the chilly autumn afternoon. "Fair enough," he said. "After all, Milk is a cat, and thus is probably going to be a shithead about 90% of the time."

"It's like you know cats or something," she said teasingly, and shot him a grin.

"Just like that," he said dryly. "Have you been over to Abby and Wyatt's house yet?"

"No, why?" she asked as he helped her up into the passenger seat of his truck. She made it all the way up and into her seat without falling on her head. Again. Two in a row. She was feeling pretty damn good about that.

"When they moved in together on July 4th, I wasn't quite sure if both Maggie Mae and Jasmine were going to live through the experience. Apparently, they spent the first month trying to murder each other."

"Did they get along like cats and dogs?" Iris asked, laughing.

"Just like that," Declan repeated, deadpan. "Maggie Mae is bigger, of course, but Jasmine is dedicated. She'd lie in wait for Maggie to come around the corner and then spring out at her. Jasmine is devious."

"I need to go over and meet this cat," Iris said. "She sounds like my kind of girl."

Declan shot her a look. "I'm not sure how I feel

about my date thinking that 'devious' is a positive trait." The quirk at the corner of his lips gave his true feelings away.

Date...

She hadn't been Declan's date since college. It was...

Nice.

Really nice.

"So are they getting along better now?" Iris asked as they headed towards Copperton, the warm air from the vents aimed directly at her. It was cozy in his truck, not a word she'd normally associate with big diesel trucks, but somehow true this afternoon.

There was something about having Declan next to her that made her feel warm and safe and comfortable.

"Yeah. I think Jasmine finally decided that she wasn't going to be able to drive Maggie away, so as long as Maggie does everything Jasmine wants, she's fine. She's finally forgiven Abby, too, for bringing her into a den filled with monsters like one friendly, obedient dog."

Iris bursted out laughing. "Now that sounds like a cat. I really want to meet her now."

"Speaking of, I've been hearing you're turning into the cat lady. I knew you've always loved cats, and of course you have Oreo and Milk, but I overheard two farmers discussing what to do with some stray cats that were showing up on their farms, and one of them said that it didn't matter; they'd all soon end up at your parents' place anyway. Are you adopting more than just Oreo and Milk?"

Iris felt her cheeks pinken a little. "No. I know I shouldn't do this because there's just no controlling it, but…I've started feeding stray cats. I accidentally busted a bag of cat food open about three weeks ago, and I cleaned up most of the mess, but it was nighttime, and I guess I missed more than I realized. Soon, there was a stray cat out there, eating the remnants in the grass. Then the next day, there was another cat. I felt bad because I'd started feeding them so I shouldn't just take the food away, you know? So then I'm putting out a couple of bowls, and…"

She grimaced. "There are a lot of stray cats in the area. I'm thinking I need to call animal control and find out about having them spayed and neutered. I just hate seeing cats not being taken care of." She bit her lower lip in consternation.

"Well, I'll text Michelle Winthrop as soon as we get to Copperton and find out if there are any programs in the area for that. She would be happy to help you out, I know it."

"Thank you!" Iris grinned at him, feeling happiness spread through her veins at his words. She'd known she couldn't continue to feed every stray cat in Long Valley County, but she also couldn't bear to see them go hungry. Some county help would be amazing.

They wound their way through the mountains until they reached Copperton, a little mountain hamlet on the road between Sawyer and Boise. It was nothing more than a wide spot in the road, really, except for the steam engine train rides they offered year-round, plus it had some great river entrances for people wanting to kayak or tube the river.

It was hard to make Sawyer feel like a bustling metropolis, but somehow, Copperton did.

Declan helped her out of the truck and they headed slowly towards the train depot. At least this was a paved parking lot, so she wouldn't have to worry about trying to make it over gravel without ending in a faceplant.

An employee met them at the door, in an old-fashioned train conductor uniform. "Sir, ma'am," he said, holding the door open wide for them. "Go on over to the ticket booth to register." He pointed to a booth set up to look like what Iris imagined a ticket booth would look like in the 1800s – black wrought iron bars, a small opening for the person behind the counter to work through, and wanted posters everywhere.

"Wow, they've really worked on this!" Iris breathed. She hadn't gone on this train ride since they were in elementary school, and they'd gone as a field trip. That had been a lot of fun, but she only vaguely remembered it. Now, as an adult, she could appreciate the work they'd gone through to make everything look and feel authentic.

"Yeah, new ownership about five years ago dumped a bunch of money into it. They're starting to advertise nationwide, trying to make this a tourist destination across the country."

"So creative," Iris said appreciatively. Why not use the history and the beauty of the area to offer specialty experiences like this? Now she wished she'd worn a skirt – a long, billowing one. It could've been fun to dress up in 1800s period clothing.

After registering, they were escorted to the waiting train where they climbed aboard. Iris held her breath, afraid she'd misjudge the steps and take a tumble but she made it up the stairs without a problem. She turned left and began heading down the aisle, which is when her foot caught and she went stumbling.

Dammit, dammit, dammit!

Of course. As soon as she stopped worrying about killing herself, that's when she fell.

But as she was falling to the wooden floor, legs and cane going everywhere, that's when Declan's strong arms went around her, catching her. "Oof!" she grunted, the air knocked out of her lungs.

Her first thought was how damn embarrassed she was. Her second thought was how damn strong Declan was.

And how good he smelled.

They froze for just a moment, her back cradled against him, his arms around her, nestled up under her breasts, and she couldn't breathe and he wasn't breathing and the world just stopped.

And then started again. He helped her stand

upright, straightening her clothing, giving her her cane back. "Are you okay?" he asked worriedly.

"Yeah, I'm fine. Just the hazards of going on a date with a cripple," she said, keeping her voice light. "Now, what booth are we in again?"

He glanced down at the rumpled ticket in his hand. "12A," he said.

She nodded brusquely and began walking again, her cheeks flaming red. Was she always going to stumble and fall in public? Was she always going to be an embarrassment to herself and those around her? If Dec had a lick of sense, he'd never ask her out again. He shouldn't. All she did was make a fool out of herself.

No reason to make a fool out of him, too.

CHAPTER 11

DECLAN

*H*E HELD HER ELBOW LIGHTLY as she slid into place in the booth and then he slid in on the other side, facing her.

Or more accurately, facing the top of her head. She seemed incredibly intent on studying the small dining room table between them. Somehow, he didn't think that she had suddenly sprouted a new interest in woodwork from the 1800s in the last three minutes.

"You're not a cripple," he said softly to the top of her head. He waited, but she didn't look up, so he finally continued. "You've been through a lot. I'm proud of you and all you've been able to do since the accident."

He dearly wanted to ask her for details about the accident, but held back. It was her story to tell. She could tell him when she felt comfortable, and until then, he'd give her the space she clearly seemed to need.

"Thanks," she said softly and then finally moved her gaze. But instead of meeting his eyes, she started looking out the window instead. It was beautiful scenery out there, for sure – stony mountains, a light dusting of snow already starting to cover the peaks, pine trees, a winding river tumbling over rocks below.

But he was pretty sure she hadn't sprouted an intense interest in the scenery in the last three minutes, either.

She began blinking rapidly, and he felt panic well up inside of him. She wasn't crying, right? He really wasn't sure what to do with a crying Iris. In their four years of dating, even when they were hiking and she fell down the side of a gulley and broke her right leg between their junior and senior year, he'd never seen her cry.

He was quite sure he didn't want to see it happen now.

A small whistle trilled, jerking their heads up in tandem. "Welcome, welcome aboard!" a conductor said up at the front of the train car. He started into his safety spiel, gesturing towards fire exits in the case of an emergency, but did it with the bored air of someone who'd done it a thousand times before.

"Enjoy the ride!" he finished. "Dinner will be served in about 30 minutes."

The steam engine whistle blew again and they started down the tracks, slowly at first, and then picking up speed as they went. Declan and Iris grinned at each other, the thrill of being on the train overriding the emotions from their earlier discussion. The murmur of voices from other passengers, the oohhs and aahhs as they went around bends, filled the air.

Yeah, taking her on this ride was such a better idea than just dinner and a movie. Who could think that this "movie" was anything less than completely amazing?

CHAPTER 12

IRIS

*H*e'd taken her hand after dinner, and the thrill that ran up her arm at his touch…

It sent shivers down her spine just remembering.

"Are you cold?" Declan asked, concerned. "I can turn the heat up if you'd like." They were on their way back to her apartment, winding through the dark, cold valley back to Sawyer.

"No, I'm okay." She squeezed his hand. It felt amazing, just sitting there, holding his hand, as if he wanted her in his life.

She couldn't begin to fathom why, but she also couldn't make herself ask him.

Speaking of things she couldn't make herself do, she couldn't make herself ask him why he'd been so hell-bent on breaking up with her all those years ago. After two weeks of telling herself that she was really going to nail him to the wall and make him talk to her, the warmth of the truck, the amazingness of holding his hand…she couldn't make herself care. At least not enough to break the spell that had been cast over them.

"That train ride was amazing. I'm so glad you thought to do that." Iris shot him a smile, and he smiled back, slow and easy…and deliciously sexy.

"Me too. I remember going in fourth grade as part of our Idaho History studies, but it's certainly a lot more special as an adult. Or, they've done a lot of work on the train since then."

"Maybe a little bit of both," Iris said softly. "Because I don't remember it being that amazing either."

What she couldn't get up the guts to say was that back then, she hadn't been holding hands with the man she'd loved for pretty much her entire life. Back in fourth grade, Declan Miller was a string-bean boy enthralled with tractors, frogs, and horses, and not necessarily in that order. If someone had told her 10-year-old self that she'd grow up to love Declan Miller, she would've laughed in their faces…and then gone on to challenge Declan to a round of H.O.R.S.E. on the basketball court, just to prove she could whoop his ass in basketball.

But when their sophomore year hit and he asked her to be his tutor in Spanish, she'd fallen head over heels in love almost instantly. It'd taken him a whole year to get up the guts to ask her out, and so she'd spent her sophomore year in a constant state of agony, asking all of her friends if they thought Declan liked her, and if he did, why didn't he ask her out, and was he flirting with another girl during lunch?

It wasn't until years later that she'd found out that he'd spent their sophomore year in an agony of nerves too, wanting to ask her out but thinking she was too beautiful for him. She snorted at the thought, jerking her back into the present.

"Whatcha thinking about?" he asked her, rubbing his thumb over her knuckles gently.

"Just how we'd spent our sophomore year liking each other but not having the guts to say so," she said with an embarrassed blush. "I should've been more bold and just told you what I was thinking. I was so shy back then."

"I never would've guessed that. You always seemed so in control, so smart. And watching you out on the court...You were a sight to behold. I figured you had every guy in school panting after you, so why would you want me?"

"Oh, on court I was a beast," she said, laughing. "No fear there. But off court? Guys were scary, especially guys named Declan Miller. They were the scariest of all."

He pulled to a stop in front of her apartment, his headlights beaming into her living room windows. Oreo, who'd been up in the window looking out, jumped down out of sight and Iris knew he'd be sitting at the door, waiting for his pettings as soon as she walked in.

"Are you still scared of men named Declan Miller?" he asked softly, turning off the engine, the sudden silence almost deafening. He picked up her hand and began kissing the knuckles, then flipped it over and began nibbling on her wrist. She sucked in a deep breath, suddenly unable to think.

"Noooo…" she stuttered out. "I think…I like them…very…much." He'd reached her inner elbow which he was softly sucking and licking. Her breath was ragged in the darkness of the cab, almost echoing through the enclosed silence.

"Turns out," he breathed against her skin, "I happen to like Iris McLains very much."

"Oh!" she said, the strangled noise erupting from her throat when he reached over and stroked her breast through her shirt. Her whole body was alive with sensations. She didn't know what she wanted or who she was.

Declan. I want Declan.

Then he was gone and it took her a moment to figure out what was going on. Her eyes shot open to find him swinging the passenger door open.

"Ma'am?" he said in a courtly voice, holding his arms out to her. She leaned into him and he scooped her up into his arms, kicking the door closed with his foot behind him as he went. He carried her down the two steps to her front door.

"You're going to hurt yourself," she mock scolded him, trying to pretend as if she really thought that. It seemed like the thing she was supposed to say, although she really couldn't bring herself to actually worry about it.

"Pshaw," he scoffed, after she reached out and turned the doorknob to let them in. "You weigh less than a baby calf does when it's born." She reached over and flipped on the light, and he gently let her slide down the front of him. She could feel his arousal straining against the fabric of his Wranglers as she slid down, and he sucked in a breath at the touch.

"Only if the calf is really, really big," she said softly, laughing up at him.

His eyes were dark with lust as he stared down at her. "Oh, some things are real big," he said with a naughty grin.

That was the last of their conversation for quite a while, as he pulled her against his chest, supporting her in his arms.

It felt so good to be home.

CHAPTER 13

DECLAN

*S*HE WAS SO RIGHT. Declan mulled over the regret he felt. They'd spent a whole year dodging around the very thing that both of them wanted. Their sophomore stupidity had nagged at Declan often over the years, almost as often as he'd regretted the choice to move up north to attend the U of I, and the loss of the intervening years.

Declan shook the thought away. This was not the night for regrets. This was a night for them. For he and Iris to finally be together the way they both longed for.

She clung to his arm tightly as they walked the few steps to her bedroom. Her grip may've had something to do with her uncertain balance, but in his mind, the tight hold she had on him was about not letting go of this chance again. His heart twinged with pleasure; he was sure she wanted this as much as he did.

And that meant everything to him.

Making it into the bedroom, she reached for the light. The overhead fixture flared to life, filling the small room with a blinding brightness. She quickly flicked on the smaller lamp on the dresser and then killed the overhead light with one smooth, practiced motion.

"I hate that damn overhead light," she said, wrinkling her nose as she turned into him. Her body felt so natural against his; they seemed to mold into each other. Declan's soul relaxed.

She bent her head slightly and pressed her face against his throat, against the beating of his heart, as he wrapped his arms around her. He felt like he could encircle her tall, slender body twice over, and protect her from the world. From all that it had thrown her way. As she snuggled a little closer, he closed his eyes and drank the moment in, wishing that he could hold onto it forever.

He bent his head to fill his nose with her sweet scent – an intoxicating mixture of shampoo and something that could only be described as *her*. Pressing his lips to the top of her head, her warmth spread through him.

The moment seemed to last forever, and yet in the blink of an eye, she stirred. Staying pinned to his body, Iris tilted her head upward with a soft whimper escaping her. In the warm glow of the lamp, he could see the need in her gorgeous blue eyes. The message was clear, and Declan could not think of a reason to deny either one of them any longer.

His lips met hers.

It was not their first kiss, of course, but the intervening years had gilded the memory of their actual first kiss. Nostalgia and regret had formed a soft haze over it, but this moment cleared away the fog of memory, joining their other first kiss in Declan's mind. As their lips moved in time with each other, rediscovering a comfortingly familiar rhythm, he reveled in the rightness of this feeling, like the satisfying click of a puzzle piece snapping into place.

Her tongue darted into his mouth and back out again, and inwardly, he grinned as his tongue chased after hers. He remembered this little signal.

His mind replayed the confusion he'd felt the first time Iris had done this. It was in the parking lot of the high school, on a crisp fall Friday night, late into the evening after a football game. They'd leaned against his beat-up truck, talking long after the lot had cleared of its students and football fans. It'd been magical – just her and him, under the garish glow of an aging street lamp. They were in their own little world – a world Declan had never wanted to leave.

Iris had cuddled into him tightly like she was right now. Their lips had met in another enchanting closed mouth kiss, but this time, he'd decided to be a little adventurous. He'd opened his mouth slightly, and her lips followed his lead.

Then...nothing. In pure dude-fashion, he didn't have a plan for what to do next.

Iris rescued him by flicking her tongue forward between his lips and then back again. His tongue instantly chased after hers. After that, their kisses became more in-depth, but each one started with her teasing him.

He pulled himself back into the present, letting his hands roam the side of her body, tracing the graceful outward turn of her hip. He let his hand rest there for a moment. She was so petite, and yet so tall. There was a reason she'd been magic on the basketball court.

He raised his hand again, letting it dip inward over her waist before moving out again until his palm cupped the side of her breast. Iris sucked in a sharp breath at his touch and pressed herself tighter to him.

The kiss was perfect in every way. Declan knew he would gladly stay in this moment for the rest of time if he could. The promise of what was going to happen next held only a small glimmer of interest compared to this feeling.

And then, it was as if they were back in high school again, with Iris stepping into her role as prompter. Pulling back just enough to separate their lips, she broke the kiss. "Come on, cowboy," she whispered, "I think it's time you paid up on a long overdue promise."

Her soft words, sweet voice, and stunning smile

worked their magic. They were just what Declan needed to keep moving forward.

He lowered his arm so that both of his arms curled around her waist. Supporting her full weight, he walked toward the bed, Iris nearly floating in time with his movement, no hesitation in her steps as they went. She was trusting him to guide her, to hold her up, to keep her from falling, and that trust made his heart twist with happiness.

Reaching the bed, he once again repositioned his arms so he was supporting her back as he slowly lowered her down. She never once stopped looking into his eyes.

Once she was fully settled in, he slipped his hands slowly from under her. His heart regretted the loss of the touch but his mind reminded him that they weren't done. He reached down and found the top button of her blouse. His thick fingers looked massive compared to the delicate enclosure.

He took his time working each of the buttons, his jeans tightening in concert with the loosening of her shirt. Each time he freed another button, more of her creamy white skin was exposed. Again, his mind flashed between the present and their youth. He recalled a tutoring session in the basement of her house that led to her lying on a couch as he fumbled with the buttons of her shirt.

The sensation of stretching denim was exactly the same.

He was happily letting himself fall into the

memory once again when a thought flashed through his mind: The memory he was re-living ended with her mother and father returning home, with Iris hurrying to re-fasten her shirt as they listened to the sound of pounding feet above them.

This time, there was no one to interrupt them.

Declan grinned with happiness to himself.

He held out his hand. Iris took it and he gently pulled her to a sitting position before pushing the soft fabric of her blouse back over her shoulders. The warm light from the lamp highlighted the flushing pink tones of her skin. His eyes followed the shallow valley between her breasts, marveling at the occasional freckle.

She struggled to free her wrists from the shirt as he leaned forward and kissed the small brown dots that complemented her porcelain skin, the heat of her body warming his face. Once again, Declan harkened back to his high school self by reaching around her with one hand and releasing the hooks of her bra. He grinned; he was much smoother in executing that particular move than he'd been so many years ago.

The black and white lace and satin bra dropped effortlessly down her arms and Declan moved his lips, drawing her nipple between them as he eased her onto the bed once more with the arm that was still wrapped around her.

Iris let out a satisfied sigh as his gentle suction pulled at her breast. That sound…this was actually happening. Finally, after the intervening years – 15 years of separation – they were going to be one again.

He took his time selfishly drinking in every sensation as his lips traversed her upper body. His head lowered to trace the swoop of her belly below her ribs. His tongue flicked a quick circle outlining her shallow navel. The fleeting touch caused her to giggle, a sound that echoed with magic and promise in his ears.

His tongue then traced a line to her hip. That spot where her jeans hid the rest of her from him. He felt her smooth skin wrinkle. Her flesh was still soft on the surface but instead of being smooth, it rose and fell beneath his lips. He pulled back just a little but before he could focus his eyes on her skin, she sucked in a quick breath and her hand pressed at the top of his head.

"That's...don't..." she stumbled, a hint of tears filling her voice as she struggled to explain.

Declan rolled to his side and reached up, taking her hand from his head and placing her palm against his lips. He kissed his way up her arm before he pulled back to look at her face. Her cheeks were a brilliant red and her eyes were panicked. She looked like she'd been backed into a corner by a dangerous snake and his heart hurt, knowing that he was the cause of that panic.

"It's okay," he whispered reassuringly, running his hand down her flushed cheek.

"This is a mistake," she bit off, the struggle to

control her emotions evident in her tone. "I'm not the same. I'm not that perfect girl anymore. I'm not what you deserve. I'm broken."

Declan drew her to him and stroked his hand down her back. He felt the tension slowly ebb as she sucked in air, her warm breath tickling his skin with each exhale.

"I'm not the same either," he said in a soft voice when he sensed her starting to calm down. "I know you have some scars, and some things are different now."

He drew in a deep breath and snuggled her closer to his side. He felt her body meld a little to his – just the tiniest give – but it gave him hope, and the courage to keep going.

"But I also know that you're the same woman who I fell in love with. Inside, you're the same woman who taught me Spanish, taught me to kiss, and taught me how to regret. I pushed you away because of my own failings. It was the worst thing I've ever done, and I've mourned that loss and cursed my stupidity every day since then. I know you're different. We all grow up and get wrinkles and gray hairs, but I need you to know that I want your scars. I want to see and I want to know because there is nothing I have ever wanted more in my life than you."

Declan's arms instinctively flexed, pulling her tighter to him, as his mind desperately hoped his physical actions would convince her of his need for her.

"I'm sorry," she said softly, finally breaking the silence. "I just ruined an amazing moment."

"No, you didn't," Declan said, and he absolutely meant it. "You made this moment amazing. If we were still kids in your parents' basement, we would've plunged forward. I never would've taken the chance to tell you how I feel. I need you to know how much I've missed you, and how much I need you to be part of my world. You gave me that chance. Thank you."

Declan knew he would never admit it out loud, but he was stunned by the blatant honesty of his own words. He didn't tend to spill his thoughts out like this, but having Iris in his arms…

He felt whole again. And brave.

"Thank you for finally saying it," she responded, craning her neck away from his body enough to capture his lips with hers. Once more, her tongue darted into his mouth and then retreated, his tongue eagerly chasing after her. As they kissed, her hand found the buttons of his shirt. Much more graceful than he could ever hope to be, she released his shirt.

Her hand was cool against his skin, her slim fingers seemingly minute compared to his broad chest.

He urged her back onto the bed. Letting their embrace end, he hurried to pull his arms free of the long sleeves. Once he was finally able to shed the damn thing, he returned to her hip. Placing his lips on the small bit of visible scar peeking out above her waistband, he explored the peaks and valleys with his tongue as his fingers fumbled with the button of her jeans.

It was an eternity before he felt the satisfying release of that button. He quickly pulled them off her, along with her socks, and then leaned back on his elbow to take her in.

Okay, he was staring. But he couldn't help himself. Naked except for the tiny patch of satin fabric that matched the bra that lay crumpled beside her on the bed, Iris was a sight to behold.

He drank her in until he couldn't resist the urge any longer, and then bent over once more to kiss her skin. Starting with the velvety skin around her ankle, he worked his way up her legs, moving from one leg to the other as he covered her with kisses.

The scars started just below her knee and ran up her right side. Light and silvery, they told him about the pain she'd gone through; the inner strength she'd had to make it through to the other side.

Declan had never thought about beauty in a philosophical way before, but as he compared the difference between her unmarred side to the other, he found himself enjoying the contrast. Something about the asymmetry of her body reminded him of life. The contrasting of the scars humanity tries to hide against the perfect bits everyone wants to show the world…it made sense to him.

How does she do it? How is it that this woman teaches me so much so easily?

"You're wearing too many clothes," she prompted once again, nudging him toward progress.

Declan pulled back, a devilish grin splitting his face. "You think so, huh?" he asked, reaching up to hook his fingers under her panties. Again, she lifted off the bed as he tugged the delicate satin down her legs. He then stood up at the end of the bed, kicking at the heels of his boots while yanking and tugging at his belt. His eyes made long, thorough sweeps of her naked body.

He felt himself harden as he took in the tuft of bright red hair that emphasized the point where her thighs met.

Finally, he got his pants and boxers off his hips and to the floor. Cursing under his breath, he snatched his jeans back off the floor and searched through the pockets until he emerged, triumphantly holding a condom aloft.

She giggled, and he decided right then and there that he'd do a lot to hear that sound again and again.

After rolling the protection in place, he hurriedly yanked his socks off, flinging them away as he placed first one knee and then the other back on the mattress. Her legs spread apart to accommodate him as he moved closer, their eyes locking with fierce need. He didn't know how much longer he could last; he was rather afraid he'd unman himself like a young randy teenager. She was so damn gorgeous…

His hands landed on each side of her shoulders and finally, he lowered his body against hers. She reached her head up to him, their lips connecting in the same moment he felt his tip press against her opening.

He stayed like that, hovering at her entrance as they kissed, until she lowered her head back onto the pillow.

"It's about damn time," she whispered with a grin.

Declan realized with a jolt that he'd been subconsciously waiting for her permission. He wanted Iris to be as sure about this as he was. With her sweet little joke he had it. Finally.

His hips flexed and he entered her in one smooth motion. Iris wrapped her arms around him and pulled herself to him, lifting herself off the bed and letting his movements lower her back down.

Their wait was finally over.

CHAPTER 14

IRIS

She awoke with a stretch and a smile. She couldn't remember what had happened to put her into such a glorious mood, until her arm whacked something warm and hard in her bed. Her eyes shot open and she jerked her head.

Oh.

Declan had happened.

He opened his eyes sleepily, smiling at her. "Good morning," he said in a deep rumble. He reached his hand out to stroke her hair away from her face. "Sleep well?"

She bit her lip, unable to hide the grin spreading over her. She couldn't remember the last time she'd woken up this happy. It was joy, pure joy, from the tips of her toes to the end of her nose.

"I may have had some pretty strenuous exercise right before falling asleep; helped me have some real amazing dreams, actually," she said with a mischievous grin.

"Funny that," he said with a matching grin. "I remember something like that, too."

He reached for her, pulling her against his chest, and began nibbling across her neck. "Hmmm... maybe we should refresh our memories..."

Just then, Iris felt a furry head whack her arm and she jerked away to find two piercing green eyes staring straight at her. "Meeowww..." Milk was hungry.

"Sorry," she said with a laugh, rolling away from a fake-pouting Declan. "If I don't feed these two, anarchy may ensue." She pulled on her ratty bathrobe and, grabbing her cane, shuffled into the kitchen to pour out the cat food for the morning. She heard Declan coming in behind her, and then over to the sink.

"If I'm going to be up, I might as well be human," he said, rinsing out the coffeepot of the remains from yesterday and refilling it. She showed him where the coffee was stored and he set about making coffee for them. It was just like their college days, and Iris couldn't help loving that feeling. Waking up next to Declan, making coffee, chit-chatting about their day ahead...

It was like the last fifteen years hadn't happened at all.

Speaking of college and studying, though...

"Hey, Dec, would you mind quizzing me on some

codes?" she asked as they settled down on the couch with their steaming mugs of coffee. Milk curled up next to her while Oreo nudged Declan's arm, hoping for some love and attention while they obviously weren't doing anything else. She grinned at her cat, shaking her head. He loved to be loved, that was for sure.

"Codes?" Declan asked, cocking his head to the side.

"Yeah, for my coding class. I'd love to have you help me run through these codes and see if I get them right."

He paused, his coffee mug partially up to his lips. "Quiz you on them?"

"Yes," she said, a little impatiently. "You know, you read the medical procedure out loud and I try to tell you which code I should use without looking at the book."

"Oh. Right. Well, I actually meant to say that I needed to get going." He scrambled to his feet, their lazy day suddenly evaporating around her. "I should've been out in the fields this morning, not lazing around in bed. Harvest is almost done, but not quite. I've got some final chores to finish up." He popped a kiss on top of her head and headed to the bedroom to pull on his clothes from last night. Before she could even push herself up to her feet, he was back in the living room. "I'll give you a call later," he promised, and then the door was closing behind him.

She collapsed back onto the couch, giving up on the struggle to stand up, and instead just stared at the front door.

"What. The. Hell," she said aloud. Why was he acting like she'd suddenly contracted some flesh-eating disease and he couldn't get out of there fast enough? She looked down at herself and then took a tentative sniff of her armpit. Did she stink? She'd taken a shower yesterday. She couldn't smell any offensive odor wafting off her, but then again, didn't they always say you couldn't smell yourself?

It couldn't have been the studying stuff. Throughout high school and college, they'd spent a lot of time studying together. He'd helped her study a lot of subjects, like…

She thought. Real hard. Had he helped her study in high school and college? Now that she thought back on it, she realized that she was always helping him. Which made sense; school came naturally to her. She didn't need much help with her classes, whereas for Declan, he usually had to work pretty hard to even get C's.

But if she needed help, like she did today, why wouldn't he be willing to help her? She didn't understand.

Just like before – he chose farming over you. Here he goes again, making that same choice. Your sister was right about him.

She pushed the thought away. Declan wasn't selfish.

He was confusing as hell, though. Someday, she'd love to figure out what was really going through that handsome head of his.

CHAPTER 15

DECLAN

He slammed his hand down on the steering wheel with a curse word that would have his mother spinning in her grave. "Dammit, Declan, you have to be better than that. *Smarter* than that." He snorted at his choice of words. "Of course, if you were smart, we wouldn't be in this predicament, would we?"

He felt a little ridiculous talking to himself out loud like this, but the last time he'd opened up to another person about this...

Well, she'd died. And if that wasn't a sign from God about keeping his big mouth shut, he didn't know what was.

"All these years, and you've managed to keep Iris in the dark about just how stupid you are," he said out loud. Because dammit all, he had no one else to talk to. He needed to get a dog like Maggie Mae, so he could at least feel less ridiculous talking out loud.

"Don't go ruining it now. No woman as smart and funny and beautiful as Iris McLain would date a dumb-as-dirt cowboy like you if she knew the truth."

He just had to get better about getting out of tight situations, was all. He'd gotten so good at it in high school and college. He could change the topic at the drop of the hat, and she never seemed to suspect a thing.

He had to relearn that ability, and fast, or he'd lose Iris.

Again.

CHAPTER 16

IRIS

"*A*RE YOU SURE they want me there?" Iris asked for the 152nd time, as they started up the lane to Wyatt's house.

Thankfully, it was nice weather today; they'd be able to spill out onto the lawn. Wyatt and Abby were in the middle of building a new home – a huge one, from what she'd heard – but it was going to be a race against the weather to get the walls and roof on before serious snow hit for the winter.

In the meanwhile, they were crammed into the Connelly family homestead, which was on the smallish side, especially with cats, dogs, and family galore filling every corner of it.

"Of course they want you here," Declan said with a reassuring smile, squeezing her hand comfortingly. "This is their big celebration day, and they want all of their friends and family here to throw a party with them."

They stopped on the side of the gravel driveway, pulling up behind some trucks and SUVs. She could hear the Mexican fiesta music from here. Declan came over to her side of the truck and helped her down. She held her breath, unsure if she was going to do a faceplant before she got to stable ground, but he lifted her down with ease, made sure she had her cane firmly in her grip, and then they set off for the house.

"So when is the adoption paperwork final?" Iris asked as they meandered along the uneven gravel road. She wanted to concentrate on walking, so she figured listening to Declan talk while they moved would keep her from having to walk and talk at the same time.

Which seemed like a damn good idea, really.

"Well, they're not sure yet. First, Wyatt had to make it through the background check, and considering what happened this past winter, that took a while."

Iris had heard that Wyatt and Abby had fallen in love while Wyatt was incarcerated at the Long Valley County Jail, but hadn't heard much more than that. She wondered if she could ask for deets without seeming like she was fishing for gossip, and finally decided that she couldn't. She'd find someone in town to give her the low-down on it.

"The sheriff's letter of recommendation was what made the difference, though. He wrote a long and glowing letter, stating that Wyatt would make a fine foster father because of all of the life experiences that he's had. Finally, my brother's propensity to get into fights was turned into a positive."

Iris couldn't help the laughter spilling out of her. It was true that Wyatt's tendency to punch first and ask questions later hadn't usually worked out in his favor. To think that his father-in-law was now supportive of him, after the bitter feud they'd had for years…

It rather made her head hurt, actually.

They finally got to the front door, and Declan knocked just once before opening it up. "We're here!" he called out.

Stetson's petite wife, Jennifer, came out of the kitchen, toting a baby on her hip. Iris had seen her at Wyatt and Abby's wedding, although no one had formally introduced them. She'd heard the story of how Stetson and Jennifer had met, of course – the Long Valley gossip chain worked just fine when it came time to tell Iris the juicy news, even if it didn't work as well when spreading the news about her.

Although it'd only been 15 months since Jennifer and Stetson had met, she already seemed like she was settling into the country lifestyle. Iris had heard that Jennifer had only worn stilettos when she'd first come to Long Valley, but today, she was wearing a pair of fun cowboy boots with turquoise leather insets.

Yeah, she seemed to be fitting right in.

Iris smiled at Jennifer, and she grinned back, open and friendly.

"You must be Iris," Jennifer said, moving to give

her a hug, and then Declan. "It's so nice to meet you, and I'm so glad you came. Abby and Wyatt are around here somewhere. Carma is in the kitchen, along with Jorge's wife, Maria. You should see everything they've got cooking." She shook her head in amazement.

Iris sniffed, loving the smells rolling out of the kitchen. It smelled divine.

"Thanks," Iris said, reaching out to stroke the fine baby hair of Jenn's baby boy. "What's his name?"

"Oh, this is Flint," Jenn said, adjusting him on her hip. "He's a momma's boy, except when he's a daddy's boy. But mostly, he's a Carmelita's boy."

They all laughed for a moment, and then Jenn said, "So, I think everyone is outside. You should head out into the backyard. I'm pretty sure Abby, Wyatt, and the guest of honor are hanging out there."

Declan guided Iris outside and over to a swinging bench seat. "Does lemonade sound good?" he asked. "Carmelita makes an amazing handmade lemonade."

"Oh, that sounds wonderful," Iris said with a huge grin. And it did. She remembered Carma from the years of going over to hang out at Declan's house in high school – she was an amazing cook, and loved all of "her" boys. She may be the housekeeper for Stetson now, but she'd been a second mother to all three of the Miller brothers.

Iris settled in and began watching the crowds in front of her. She used to want to be in the middle of every gathering, every group, because she was so social. She still loved people, but…she wasn't sure if it was the uncertainty of not knowing if her balance would be quite right and she might take a tumble at any point or what, but she was a lot more content to simply…be.

She watched Juan as he played with Jorge's grandchildren. Jorge was Wyatt's foreman, and he had about 700 grandkids, from what Iris could tell. Okay, not really that many, but quite a few. Wyatt had bonded with Juan while he was working at Adam's therapy camp, and tonight was a celebration of being able to bring Juan home with them. He'd been living at a foster home here in Sawyer but Wyatt and Abby put in to be foster adopt parents, rather than just foster parents, and so the courts agreed to let him move in with them.

Wyatt went walking over to the group of kids playing soccer and called out to Juan. He came trotting over, a grin on his face, and they chatted for a moment. Seeing Wyatt as a father…It made Iris tingle with happiness. He deserved to find happiness. Iris had never met his daughter Sierra, but she knew that losing her to that drunk driver all those years ago had wounded him in a way that no one thought he'd ever recover from.

Seeing him now did the soul some good.

Declan came jogging up, a lemonade in each hand. "Sorry that took so long," he said with a smile as he held hers out. "I got shanghaied into setting up some tables."

She accepted it gratefully and took a deep sip. "Oh wow," she said after she swallowed the mouthful of sunshine and tartness that was the lemonade. "I've never had such a wonderful lemonade in all my life."

"Isn't it amazing?" Declan shook his head with a grin. "I could take cooking lessons for the rest of my life and never whip up the kinds of dishes that Carmelita seems to make without blinking."

Jennifer came out of the back door holding Flint. "Hey Dec, Carmelita is needing another table set up for the food." She leaned in closer and whispered conspiratorially, "I think she's afraid the other one is going to buckle under the weight of all this food."

Declan laughed and whispered back, "I think she's probably right." He straightened up. "I'd hate to have her food go to waste. I'll be right back." He popped Iris a kiss on top of her head and headed back inside.

Jennifer slipped onto the bench next to Iris. "So, you and Declan," she said with a grin, nudging Iris in the ribs. "Do tell."

Iris had to laugh at the blunt desire for gossip. Jennifer was nothing if not clear about what she wanted. "I'm not sure if there's much to tell," she said with a shrug. "We used to date in high school and the first two years of college, and now…Well, I'm not really sure what we're doing, to be honest."

Abby came walking up, an easy smile on her face. "I heard that last part," she called out, grabbing a chair and settling herself down across from Iris and Jenn. "You two were a year ahead of me in school, but I remember how cute I thought you two were back then. I was so surprised to hear you'd broken up."

Abby and Jenn looked at her expectantly. They wanted the deets, but Iris wasn't really sure about them herself.

"I know this sounds weird, but I honestly am not sure what happened back then." She shrugged helplessly. "Things were going great, and I thought he was going to propose. We'd discussed marriage, but it had always been a, 'After we graduate from college' sort of thing. And then, his mom died in that awful car wreck, and he just completely changed. Overnight, really. It wasn't too much after that that he told me he wanted to go to the U of I and he wanted to break up with me. He maintained it was because they had a better agriculture program up there, which is true of course, but he hadn't cared about that the first two years of college. Why did he suddenly care about it the second two years of college?"

She heaved a sigh. "I had a scholarship to ISU. I couldn't afford to leave it and go to the U of I with him. He knew that. That's why we decided together to go to ISU. And then suddenly, it wasn't good enough for him." She smiled but she knew she wasn't convincing anyone with it. The memory still hurt. She still needed to get him to tell her why. She still needed to grow a backbone and demand some answers.

She still didn't want to. The life she was enjoying

right now with him seemed too fragile. Like a bubble that could pop at any moment.

She didn't have the guts to test that theory.

Something she wasn't too proud of, honestly.

Flint started gurgling, interrupting their little confab, and Jennifer grinned at her, apparently understanding Iris' need to change the topic of conversation, and said, "I think Flint would love some time with you. Want to hold him?"

"Oh yes," Iris breathed happily. She was grateful she was sitting down so she didn't have to worry about dropping him on his head or something. Just the thought sent a bolt of panic through her, but snuggling Flint against her quickly made the panic dissipate. "Jennifer, he's so beautiful. How old is he?"

"Six months. And his eyes are already starting to change. I think he's going to end up with brown eyes? It's hard to tell right now. Anyway, you can already tell he's got Stetson's jaw."

It was true. Especially for a baby, Flint's jaw was square. He was going to be a heartbreaker when he grew up. He kicked his legs and grinned at her, obviously proud of himself for making his legs kick when he wanted them to. "Such a handsome boy," Iris cooed.

Carmelita, Stetson and Jennifer's housekeeper and cook extraordinaire, came out onto the back porch. "Oh, I did not see you come in," she said to Iris in her light Hispanic accent. "It is good to see Declan here with such a beautiful woman." Carma winked at her and Iris blushed. It was times like this that she really hated having such light skin. She was probably glowing brilliant red right now.

"You want to tell everyone it is time to eat?" Carmelita asked, turning towards Abby. "I cannot keep the children's fingers out of the food any longer anyway. I keep whacking them with my wooden spoon but they do not seem to notice." Carma's eyes crinkled up at the corners, and Iris knew she was joking.

"Especially the taller children?" Iris asked dryly, bouncing Flint on her lap. He laughed with joy.

"*Especially* the taller children," Carmelita confirmed. "The tallest ones are the worst."

They all laughed for a moment, and then Carma headed back inside. Jennifer held her arms out for Flint and with a sigh, Iris handed him back. He was quite possibly the cutest drool monster she'd ever laid eyes on. Abby headed over to the pick-up soccer game and hollered, "C'mon you guys, it's eating time!" The kids cheered and instantly dropped the soccer ball in favor of heading to the back porch. The smells coming from the kitchen had obviously been tempting everyone for quite a while.

Iris watched as everyone queued up, moving past the buffet tables groaning under the weight of the food. Suddenly, she felt Declan drop a kiss on top of her head and she looked up, startled. "Oh hey!" she said.

"Hi, Cookie." She blushed at his use of his old

nickname for her. He'd given it to her when she'd gorged on Chips Ahoy one night, eating an entire box by herself. She still remembered how much her stomach hurt from that escapade. "I was going to go through the line for us. Is that okay? You can hold down the fort over here."

"Sure, that'd be great." Iris had been waiting for the line to die down before she went through because she hadn't wanted to stand forever while waiting, but having Declan go through instead, so she didn't have to try to juggle her cane, a plate, and a serving spoon at the same time…

It was lovely, really.

"Great. Be right back." He jogged off to the end of the line, where he started chatting with one of Jorge's kids. Iris watched him for a moment – strong, tall, thoughtful – and suddenly wondered what on earth he was doing with her. He had this amazing family, he had a farm, he had a successful life. He didn't need her with her special needs and her damn canes.

No one needed her. Not anymore. Not like they did before, when she was a nurse and could help others. Now she was the hopeless one.

And it was slowly starting to drive her insane.

CHAPTER 17

DECLAN

He stared down at the loan document in front of him. God, he hated reading. He hated paperwork.

He especially hated reading paperwork.

He closed his eyes and rubbed them hard with the palms of his hands. If he just concentrated hard enough, he'd be able to read this. He could make it happen.

He opened up his eyes and stared down at the loan paperwork. The words swum around, letters going every which way.

He went back up to the top and started with the first word. "This."

Okay, this was good. He was making progress. One word at a time. That was his mantra. He could read any document, one word at a time.

He struggled to the end of the first (stupidly long and convoluted) sentence and realized he was covered in sweat. He might as well have run a marathon. He would've at least had the endorphins from the exercise.

As it was, he just felt like shit.

He sat back in his chair with a groan. A large part of him just wanted to give up and sign the damn things. He needed seed for next year. He needed to upgrade his combine; his current one barely made it through the season. Declan had never been as happy as he was to see the combine drive off the field one last time. It'd made it through, helped along by a lot of cursing, oil, and thumping with a wrench.

He didn't want to upgrade, of course. The newer ones had enough features on them that he was quite afraid that if he pushed the wrong damn button, he'd launch a rocket ship into space. He didn't need GPS and a seat warmer and a back massager built in.

Realizing that even he couldn't make his current combine last another year, though, he'd spent yesterday talking with Moose Garrett down at the John Deere dealership, picking out a stripped-down model that, you know, *harvested wheat*.

No rocket ships or back massagers included.

But now came the dreaded part: The loan paperwork from the credit union. He opened up his eyes and glared at the papers spread across his dining room table. His father had taught him how to grow crops and by God, Declan Miller could grow crops. He learned all he needed to know from his dad on the topic, and if he had any questions, he could always ask a seed salesman for help and ideas.

But loan paperwork? His dad hadn't taught him some simple work around for it. He was stuck with it, whether or not he wanted to be. Whether or not he could even read it.

He toyed with the idea of calling Stetson or Wyatt. They didn't know that he could barely read, of course. That wasn't something that you just went around telling everyone.

Or, in Declan's case, that he went around telling anyone. Anyone ever, except his beloved mother.

And look at how that turned out.

The idea of telling his brothers he needed help made his stomach clench with a toxic combination of fear and panic. A real man just did what he needed to do. A real man didn't need help reading his damn loan paperwork.

A real man didn't have dyslexia.

Of course, Declan didn't know for sure if he did. He'd made sure to stay far, far away from any tests that would have diagnosed him as such. It was bad enough to guess he had dyslexia. It'd be so much worse to know.

He'd made it through school by the skin of his teeth. And through the help of Iris, although of course she didn't know either. The idea of telling her sent ice thrumming through his veins. That was a terrifying idea. He figured he'd rather swallow hot lava than tell Iris that the man she'd loved and dated for so long was dumb as a pile of rocks. She was so damn smart; valedictorian of their class. Scholarship to Idaho State University. Top scores on her SAT. If she knew the truth about him…?

Well, he just wouldn't let it happen. Ever.

He had a second chance with Iris. He'd been stupid before, letting the panic and pain of losing his mom affect him so irrationally. He wouldn't be stupid again.

Well, at least not stupid when it came to giving up Iris. He was obviously stuck with the stupidity of not being able to read. That was a condition that he was stuck with for life.

The best he could do was make sure no one ever knew.

He sat up, grabbed his pen, and signed the paperwork at the bottom. Whatever it said, he'd just have to live with it. He'd used Georgia down at the credit union for a couple of years now. He'd trusted her thus far. What was one more loan?

He shoved the paperwork into an envelope and stood up. Time to deliver it to the Goldfork Credit Union and cross his fingers that he wasn't getting screwed over.

If he wanted to be a farmer, he didn't have any other choice. And really, what else was he going to be? An employer would expect him to be able to read, so it wasn't like he could go to work for someone else.

And if he wanted to raise farm animals instead – like pigs; oh, how he wanted to raise pigs! – he'd have to figure out how to deworm them and feed them and how to buy a sow and how to breed them and when to take them to the butchers and…

Impossible. Just impossible. The idea of that much reading made his right eye twitch with panic.

He was a row crop farmer for life, and that's all there was to it. He had no other choice.

CHAPTER 18

IRIS

*I*RIS PULLED TO A STOP in front of the optometrists and stared up at the cheerful sign – Mor-Vision, with the slogan, *Don't you want to see mor…?* emblazoned below it.

She didn't want to be there. She rather figured she would choose to be anywhere but there if she could get away with it.

It wasn't that she minded Dr. Mor. He was fine and all. He gave her her first eye exam when she was ten; helped fit her for her first pair of glasses when she was fifteen. She'd long ago started wearing contacts, and he'd fitted her for those, too.

No, it wasn't Dr. Mor, or even the idea of spending money on glasses, although God knows she didn't have much room left in the budget for them. Spending significant amounts of time in the ICU at the hospital with a brain injury did tend to put a damper on checkbook balances.

No, it was the idea that she was about to admit defeat. And she really, really hated to admit defeat.

She was pretty sure she was going to break out into hives simply by walking through the front door of the Mor-Vision.

She made herself climb out of her car and slowly make her way up to the front door of the business.

I can do this. I can do this.

What if he says you can't be a medical coder anymore?

Too damn bad. I'm going to be one anyway.

Nothing like getting into a knockdown, drag-out fight with yourself...and losing.

She pushed the glass door open and the doorbell tinkled, alerting Mrs. Mor to her presence. Dr. Mor and his wife had worked together in the same office for coming up on fifty years. Iris figured that meant that someone somewhere deserved a medal, if only because they'd managed not to kill each other in all that time.

"Hi, Iris!" Mrs. Mor said with a warm smile. "Nice to see you back at home, dear." Her eyes skittered to Iris' cane and back up to her face, but she thoughtfully kept mum on that topic. "I'll tell Dr. Mor you're here." She stood up with a sweet smile to Iris, turned toward the examination room, and bellowed, "Iris is here! Where are you?!" She turned back around and gave another sweet smile to Iris.

"He'll be right along," she said pleasantly, as if Iris couldn't hear everything that had just happened.

Iris did her best to hold in her giggles and just

forced a pleasant smile instead. Inside, she was dying with laughter. She figured that if a couple worked together for 50 years, maybe they deserved an eccentric habit…or seven.

She relaxed a little bit, the panic she'd been feeling out in the car de-escalating from nuclear meltdown to low-pitched pulsing. Being back in here was a bit like coming home. Some things really didn't change.

"Iris," Dr. Mor said, coming out of the exam room with a warm smile on his face. "So good to see you, dear." She noticed that they'd both called her "dear." She wondered if that also came with the territory of working together for years on end – the same nickname for everyone. "Come on back."

He held the door open for her as she maneuvered into the room, past him and into a waiting chair. She sank down into it with a happy sigh. It never failed to surprise her how exhausting it was to move. She remembered working twelve-hour shifts in the ICU, hardly sitting down for a break, and thriving on it.

That Iris was long gone.

He sat across from her, his long tufts of white hair sticking out every which direction from his head. She wondered why Mrs. Mor wasn't in there, combing his hair down. She was always fussing over him but today…he looked a little more frazzled than normal.

"I heard that you got in a car wreck," he said, with a nod towards her cane. "Is that where that came from?"

She nodded. "I've been out of the hospital for about six weeks. Mom and Dad moved me into that little apartment behind their house."

"That's a good call. Good to have someone who can watch over you in case something happens. Now, is it damage to your leg or spine that is causing you to need a cane, or something else?"

"Something else. I have a traumatic brain injury that affects the nerves in my head," she swirled a hand around her head, as if Dr. Mor couldn't locate it on his own, "and keeps the messages from my feet from reaching my brain, basically. The technical term is *sensory impairment*, but the long and short of it is, I have to retrain my brain to rely on my eyesight and my inner ear for balance, rather than on being able to tell what's going on because my feet are telling me what I'm doing." She shrugged. "The doctors think that I'll get better over time, but…it's been a slow slog."

"Are you doing physical therapy?" he asked.

"Yes. Thankfully, they're able to send a nurse down here to the Long Valley Clinic twice a week so I don't have to drive to Boise for it."

She wasn't sure what she would've done if she'd had to make the 90-minute drive to Boise twice a week. She only just barely trusted herself to drive across town to the optometrist and to the grocery store. The long, windy road to Boise?

No way.

"Good, good. So, tell me why you're in here today. Are you wanting a full eye exam? Are you thinking your prescription may have changed because of the accident?"

She shifted in her chair uncomfortably. Despite his kindly voice and his oversized ears that had caused her to nickname him Dr. Dumbo until her mom heard her and washed her mouth out with soap, she wanted nothing more than to make a run for the door.

Or at least a really fast waddle.

"My eyes have been hurting a lot," she said carefully. "I wasn't sure if the prescription had changed, or something else."

"Are you squinting in order to read books close up, or at signs far away?"

She shook her head.

"Are your eyes just aching, like you've been working them pretty hard?"

She slowly nodded her head. *Dammit, dammit, dammit.*

It was like he'd been an eye doctor for fifty years or something.

Just like that.

"I see," he said noncommittally. "You're wearing glasses today, but you usually wear contacts. Are you wearing the glasses because of your eyes hurting?"

"No, I just thought they'd be easier to remove for an eye exam." She pushed the bulky glasses up her nose. Other people could make coke-bottle glasses adorable, she was sure.

She just wasn't one of those people.

"Let's go ahead and do that exam now and see where we're at. Take off your glasses and put them on the counter."

He quickly and efficiently ran her through the exam, asking her endless rounds of "Which one looks better – this one or this one?"

Finally, he sat back and looked at her straight on.

"Iris, I think you're pushing yourself too hard after your accident." She opened up her mouth to protest, but he held up his hand to stop her excuses and explanations trembling on the tip of her tongue. "Are you going to school? Working? What are you doing to keep yourself busy every day?"

Drooling over Declan Miller.

The thought popped into her head and she bit back a groan at herself. Now was not the time to go off into la-la land.

"I am almost done with my classes through Hermingston Medical College. I'm becoming a medical coder through their online program."

"Weren't you an RN before the accident?" he asked, his brow wrinkling as he tried to remember back.

"Yeah, so I figured being a medical coder would at least use my medical knowledge, plus I can do it from home."

"A smart choice. Except, Iris, I'm afraid the computer screen is hard on your eyes. Have you been staring at a screen a lot lately?"

She nodded so slowly, someone might be forgiven

for thinking that she was simply moving her head around casually.

He was even better than she'd feared he'd be.

"How long have you been enrolled in this course?"

"About four weeks."

He settled back in his overstuffed antique office chair with a sigh. "Iris, the problem is that if you continue to strain your eyes like this, you could cause permanent damage to them. With a brain injury, you aren't capable of working an 8-hour day like other people can. At least, not right now, and certainly not if that 8-hour day includes a lot of screen time."

And then, it happened. What she'd feared. What she hadn't wanted anyone to say to her, ever.

"Have you thought about going on to disability? At least for the short term? Then your body could recuperate. I would be happy to write—"

"No, thank you, Dr. Mor," she broke in. She normally would never interrupt someone like that, at least not an elder, but she didn't want him to say it.

She didn't want to hear it.

"I just came today because I need to know if there's a trick I can use."

"A trick?" He stared at her as if she'd sprouted a limerick in ancient Greek.

"Yes. You know, some way for me to not get eye strain from staring at a computer." She'd googled that question but none of the suggestions had worked. She figured if anyone knew a special trick, it'd be Dr. Mor.

"Don't stare at a computer so much," he said bluntly. "Iris, your eye strain isn't a case of ordinary eye strain. It's stemming from your brain injury. The harder you push your body, the worse it'll get. The trick is to not push your body."

She nodded stupidly and then grabbed her cane to push herself to her feet. She had to go. She had to go right then. She couldn't quite breathe right and there was definitely dust in the air, because somehow both of her eyes were irritated and filling with tears.

Damn dust.

"Thanks, Dr. Mor," she said around the lump in her throat. She cleared it impatiently. The dust level was getting out of control, truly. Now it was causing large lumps in her throat. "I'll keep that in mind."

And then she turned and limped towards the door, moving as fast as her off-kilter mind and off-kilter body would allow her to.

Which wasn't nearly as fast as she wanted to move.

CHAPTER 19

DECLAN

*D*ECLAN KNOCKED on the door and then stepped back, a grin on his face. Iris was going to love today's present.

She opened the door and he held up a large paper bag. "Fresh catnip," he said proudly, in lieu of a greeting. "My neighbor has a patch that is out of control, and the neighborhood cats all seem to think that her flowerbed is their new home. She practically threw the catnip at me and told me to make a run for the truck."

Iris bursted out laughing, and Declan felt pride and happiness swell in his chest. He'd made her laugh. He felt ten feet tall.

She stood back and let him past her and into the apartment, closing the door behind him quickly. "It's getting to be that time of year," she said, burrowing down into her sweater. "I can't believe Halloween is almost here."

"Which just means that it's a perfect time for us to go to the Harvest Festival together."

Just then, Oreo and Milk came streaking out of one of the back bedrooms and came to a stop in front of him, their eyes staring up at him eagerly.

"It's like they know that's catnip," Iris said dryly.

"Yeah, just like that," he said with a grin. "You two ready to become very, very happy?" He took the catnip out and sprinkled it on the floor, and they began rolling around in it ecstatically. "I think I'm making your cats high," he said with a wink at her. She blushed, and he figured that was just as good of an invitation as any to get a hello kiss. "While the kids are occupied," he said in a low growl, and wrapped his arms around her waist, pulling her to him. She melted into his arms and tilted her head up, offering her sweet lips to him.

As their lips melded together, moving with an urgency that made...certain parts of him south of the belt line come alive, he wondered anew at finding Iris again. Having her in his life again. Her brilliant red hair brushed his shoulders and he breathed in deeply. She smelled so damn good.

He wondered if she realized how beautiful she was.

Knowing her, probably not.

Finally, he forced himself to pull away and instead contented himself with nestling her against his thighs. She felt so perfect in his arms.

While the cats yowled and purred their way

through the pile of catnip, he sniffed the air. It smelled…off. He pulled away from Iris and breathed in deeply. "Are you…cooking something?" he asked hesitantly. Iris had never been much of a cook, but that sure smelled like snickerdoodles.

Burnt snickerdoodles, if his nose was correct.

"Oh noooooo!" she wailed, yanking away from him and hurrying to the kitchen, using furniture along the way for support. "I was going to set the timer, and then…"

She yanked the oven door open and the smell hit at the same time as the sight of dark smoke curling out. Choking, he ran over to the window above the kitchen sink and yanked it open, then searched for the fan switch over the range. He flipped it on high, then turned back to see Iris, hands on hips, glaring at the oven. It was a good thing looks couldn't kill, or he was plenty sure the oven would go up in flames, with the strength of that glare.

Of course, if she continued to keep cooking, the oven might go up in flames anyway…

He couldn't help himself – the laughter he'd been holding in came busting out. She looked up, shooting death rays at him too, and then…she broke. Her lips twitched, one corner and then the other, and then she began laughing also.

"Oh Declan," she said, between gales of laughter, "how is it that I can be so smart, and yet so stupid at the same time? How hard is it to set a timer?!"

If Iris Blue McLain was anything at all, it wasn't

stupid. She had more book smarts in her little pinky than he did in his whole body.

Street smarts, on the other hand…

He decided to sidetrack her from her train of thought by scooping her up into his arms and carrying her to the couch, matching the squeal of her surprised laughter with a grin of his own.

He settled down on the couch, cradling her in his arms. The way she was squirming around on his lap meant he was going to be very interested in something other than her complete inability to cook in just a minute, but he tried to stay focused on the topic at hand.

No matter how tempting it was to just stare at her pink, soft lips.

"So why did you skip setting a timer?" he asked, once she'd finally stopped laughing. He wasn't about to pour salt into an open wound and say it out loud, but it did seem like a plenty easy thing to do.

"I got sidetracked reading," she said meekly, like she was confessing to a triple homicide. She was completely embarrassed.

He was completely enchanted.

"Andddd…" he prompted, when that appeared to be the end of her explanation.

"I thought I'd just read for a minute. That minute became a really long minute."

He threw his head back with a hearty chuckle, the fun of lightly teasing Iris almost outweighing the pain of discussing reading. "Anything in particular that you were reading?"

"A romance novel. Julia Quinn. She's my favorite historical author."

"Hmmm…" Declan's mind had wandered from the topic because…well, it was reading, for one, but even more importantly, Iris was sitting on his lap. Suffice it to say, the blood in his body was not in his brain. His hand wandered up under her shirt, stroking the soft bare skin of her back.

She felt amazing.

"Well, we better get going before the festival ends without us!" she said brightly, wiggling off his lap and to her feet.

Had she wiggled a little more than she'd needed to, to get off his lap? He was pretty sure she had. She looked over at him and just smiled innocently.

He didn't trust that innocent smile – not one bit.

He figured he was being damn smart not to.

She grabbed her cane from the corner – a wooden staff with intricate swirls, topped with a funky head. Her hand fit into the grip and he realized that it was a specialized grip made just for her. Or at least a hand close to her size.

He'd never seen anything quite like it. "Where did you get that cane from?" he asked, helping her into her jacket draped over the end of the couch.

"Ohhh…uhhh…"

She was back to blushing again.

One of the best things about dating Iris McLain

in high school and college was that she never hid a single emotion on her face. She was an open book. It made watching her endlessly fascinating, like watching a play where turning away for just a moment meant missing minute details and insights into what she was thinking.

They strolled together towards the front door, and he called out to the cats, who were busy cleaning each other from their catnip bath, "You two stay out of trouble. Now," he said, turning back to Iris on his arm, "Miss McLain, spill the beans. What's up with your cane?"

"I made it," she said in a rush.

That stopped him in his tracks. "Really?" he asked, stunned. "I had no idea you knew how to do that sort of thing."

She shrugged and started walking forward again, obviously uncomfortable with his praise. He opened the front door and they began their slow amble towards his truck. "Well, I decided to figure it out. Those black orthopedic canes with the four feet sprouting out of the bottom? No way. Not for me. My body may think that I'm 90 years old, but that doesn't mean I have to dress like it. So I had my parents bring some books home for me from the library and I started studying them. There are some really amazing canes out there."

Books. She taught herself how to make canes by reading books.

He didn't know why that fact bothered him so

much. He shouldn't be surprised. She was so damn smart, she read books for fun, something he had no concept of.

He just smiled and held open the door of his truck for her, helping her in and then hurrying around to the other side. He couldn't let her see how much her explanation affected him. He couldn't make her injury all about him. Especially because it was all about the stupid him, the one where letters didn't stay put and books were torture devices.

Casting about for something to talk about, anything that didn't involve books, he blurted out, "So you never told me how this happened." He waved his hand around in the air, gesturing to her whole body, but inside, he was panicking. He'd told himself not to ask; to let her bring it up when she felt comfortable. Now that he was desperate to change topics, he was pushing her for answers when she'd been staying far away from the subject.

He wasn't being fair, and he knew it.

He couldn't seem to stop himself, though.

"Oh, I haven't?" She let out a high-pitched laugh that was uncomfortable and awkward as hell. "I guess I didn't realize that." The tips of her ears were a brilliant pink, which was Sign #1 that she was lying her ass off to him. Iris never could lie worth a damn. He opened up his mouth to apologize for bringing it up, but she kept talking in a rush, keeping him from saying anything.

"I was driving home from the hospital after an 18-

hour shift in the ICU. There'd been a bad wreck that day – three-car pile-up – and I was exhausted. We'd had a nurse call in sick so we'd been short-staffed, and then the wreck meant that the ICU had been packed. Pocatello isn't as small as Sawyer, of course, but we're nothing like Boise or Salt Lake.

"Anyway, I saw something out of the corner of my eye but my reflexes were too slow. By the time I realized the herd of deer was crossing the freeway, I was already plowing into them. I killed two deer that night." Her voice had dropped to a mere whisper, and her knuckles were white, gripping together. She looked like she was holding on for dear life…with herself. "I don't remember much after that for almost a week. It's just gone." She shrugged, staring at the country road ahead of them.

Deer. She hit deer.

His mind flashed back to his mother's vehicle. He'd been the one tasked with managing the disposal of the vehicle after her accident, and the bloated carcass of the animal that had killed her…

He swallowed hard, feeling the palms of his hands grow sweaty.

Breathe, just breathe.

"I'm really glad you're okay," he said softly, reaching over and patting her hand. She grabbed his hand with surprising strength, clinging to it like it was her lifeline.

And maybe it was.

"Thanks," she said softly. "I don't like to talk

about it – that accident took so much away from me. I don't think I'd told anyone the full story before now. I wish I could say that I feel better, now that it's out of me, but…I mostly just feel afraid. What if it happens again? What if this time, it kills me? Like it did your mom?" *Keep a straight face. Just nod. Don't show your reaction.* "And, I killed two other beautiful animals. If I'd been more alert, I might've been able to slow down or swerve or something. Instead, I just plowed right into them…" Her voice cracked, and he squeezed her hand, his heart breaking right along with her.

It felt like someone had taken his heart out and was wringing it dry.

"Anyway," she said in a happier tone that rang with false brightness, "Mom and Dad are encouraging me to go to a counselor, and I probably should. I keep telling myself that just talking about it won't actually kill me, even if it feels like it will."

They'd long ago pulled to a stop in front of the city park, the Harvest Festival in full swing around them. He squeezed her hand, listening to the silence, waiting to see if she wanted to say anything more. He'd forced her to speak about it; it was only right that he let her tell him everything she wanted to say.

Finally, when it became clear she had nothing else to share, he cleared his throat and asked softly, "Are you okay to go out there and mingle with the fine folk of Sawyer? If you want me to take you back home, that's no problem."

She turned to him, a forced smile on her face. "No, of course not! We're here. Let's go have some fun."

He raised her knuckles to his mouth and brushed them against his lips. God, he loved this woman. Even if he didn't deserve her, he couldn't make himself give her up.

CHAPTER 20

IRIS

*S*HE WAITED FOR HIM to come around to her side of the truck to help her out, her insides jelly. She was surprised by how hard it'd been for her to tell him about the accident. She'd been avoiding it on purpose, of course, so it shouldn't have been surprising that it was rough to talk about, but still, it was even worse than she'd thought it was going to be.

Strange as it sounded, it was the week after the accident that was just a giant black void in her brain that scared her the most. Try as she might, she couldn't remember any of it. She wanted to. She lay awake in bed and tortured herself with that time period again and again.

But it was just gone.

Which was freaky as hell. She couldn't imagine how shaken she would've been to wake up without any memory at all. That thought was even more terrifying.

Declan opened up the door and helped her down, getting her situated with her cane before closing the door behind her and they started off towards the festival. She smiled up at him, forcing her fears and pain down deep inside of her. She was with Declan Miller, the man she'd loved since the 10th grade. She wasn't about to waste time reliving the worst night of her life. She had better things to do – like flirt with Declan Miller.

"So what are we going to hit first?" she asked, glancing around the city park. A small train, pulled by a four-wheeler, whizzed past, small children in the "train cars" grinning with excitement. She wished she could fit into one of those cars. Alas, she was about 30 years too old for it.

"Are you hungry?" he asked. "We could find food first, or just wander around. Or…" He got a slightly panicked look on his face. "Ummm…would you rather just sit? I can bring things to you." He looked awkward as hell, and she wanted to put him out of his misery as quickly as possible.

"No, I'm fine. As long as I have my cane in one hand and my other arm through yours, I'm okay. It's good for me to walk around." She wouldn't be able to do so forever, but dammit all, she'd do it as long as she could. She was sick and tired of being an invalid. And sick and tired of sitting all the time. "Let's go look at the animals. They're my favorite part." Of course. He knew that – it was always her favorite part.

He grinned down at her and said, "Some things never change."

She grinned back. "You know it, babe."

They wandered over to the soccer field, where pens were set up to hold the animals during the festival. Most of the animals were at full weight, there to be bid upon. But between the rows of full-sized sows and cows, Iris spotted a litter of piglets. "Ohh!" she squealed, and began tugging Declan towards them, as fast as her body would allow her to go. "Look, Declan, they're adorable!"

A gentleman appeared, and it took Iris a moment to recognize him. It was Mr. Harther, a local specialty pig farmer.

"Hi, Mr. Harther," Declan said, putting his free hand out to shake. They chatted for a moment about the amazing weather they were enjoying, considering the time of year, and then Iris' patience was gone.

"So why do you have piglets in October?" she asked, breaking into their discussion of the occurrence of strong winds in the valley in the fall.

"Well now, that'd be me not keeping strong enough fences," he said with a bemused smile on his face. "There's that saying – where there's a will, there's a way, and well...I guess there was a will!" His weathered face got a little pink and Iris tried to hide her grin at the farmer's embarrassment at discussing sex with her, even if it was of the porcine variety.

Declan slipped his arm out from under Iris' and leaned over the enclosure, scratching one of the piglets under their chin. The baby pig closed its eyes and sighed with obvious pleasure.

"I woke up one morning," the farmer continued, "to find the boar had burrowed his way into the sow's pen and had made himself at home. She was supposed to become someone's bacon and ham supply this winter, but once this happened," he gestured at the pen in front of them, "I realized that plan was off the table. I know you raise wheat, Declan," he said, turning to him, "but you've always had a way with animals. If you ever decide to switch over to pig farming, let me know. I can get you started with your own herd."

Iris held on to the enclosure for balance, watching as Declan played with the piglets. They tumbled over and around each other like small puppies, fighting for milk from their mama, or for attention from Declan. Their squeals filled the air. Iris thought it was just about the most adorable thing she'd ever seen.

"Oh no sir!" Declan exclaimed, straightening up quickly. His back was ramrod straight as he looked at Mr. Harther. "Millers are row crop farmers. We've been here since the 1800s. We don't raise anything else. That's the way it is, and that's the way it's always gonna be."

His voice was strident, forceful, and the speech was a little on the…practiced side? Iris stared at him, working through the possibilities. Why was Declan acting so weird about such a simple and friendly offer?

"I just thought I'd let you know it was an option," the older farmer said, raising his hands in mock surrender. "No need to get worried about it. I just thought you were a natural. Always have. Well, anyway, I best be getting the missus and I some lunch. You two enjoy the piglets." He turned and headed towards the food wagons lining the sidewalk running through the middle of the park.

Iris elbowed him hard in the ribs.

"Oww!" Declan said, rubbing his side. "What was that for?"

"What was that speech for?" she demanded. "You acted like he asked for your first-born child."

He shrugged nonchalantly. "There's just no use discussing such a thing. I'll admit that pigs are my favorite animal, but…well, you heard me. Millers raise wheat and corn and hay, not animals."

"Stetson raises cows," Iris pointed out in her very best 'I am acting patient with you even though I want to hit you over the head for being stubborn' voice.

"Stetson's always been the one to do things differently. Not everyone gets to be Stetson. You ready for an elephant's ear?" he asked in a transparent bid to change the topic that was so obvious, a five year old would've spotted it.

"Sure," she murmured, and then made her way over to a wide open spot in the grass and collapsed into a heap. She'd worn herself out, standing so dadblamed much, and her leg muscles and eyes were straining from the exercise. As she watched Declan wind his way over to the food vendors, she repeated his words in her head.

Not everyone gets to be Stetson…not everyone gets to be Stetson…

The hell of it was, she had no idea what that meant.

And she wasn't sure she was brave enough to push him for an answer.

CHAPTER 21

DECLAN

*D*ECLAN DROVE to Iris' apartment, his thumbs beating on the steering wheel in time with the upbeat country music twanging from the radio. It'd been two weeks since Iris had graduated from Hermingston and one week since she'd started working for the Portneuf Medical Center as a coder. They'd been sad to lose her as a nurse, of course, which meant that when she'd come back to them and applied for the job of a work-from-home coder, they were thrilled to bring her back.

Declan was as proud of her as if he'd done it all himself. Which of course he hadn't. He never could. Maybe that was why he was so proud of her.

Either way, he was ready to take her out for dinner tonight to celebrate her victory. After all she'd gone through, for her to do as well as she was…well, it was a miracle. That's all there was to it. She sure was something.

He bounded out of his truck, a package tucked under his arm. He'd asked the lady down at the store to wrap it up for him so it'd look nice, and not just be wrapped up in the Sunday comics like it would've been if he'd been put in charge of that part of the process. Thank God all he had to do was pick the damn thing out and hand over his credit card. He figured that was a pretty fair trade.

She opened up the door and he grinned as he held up the box for her to see.

"You know, you're going to spoil me if you keep buying me presents every time you pick me up for a date," she said scoldingly, but the huge grin on her face belied her words, as did her reaching eagerly for the package.

He held it out of her reach with a teasing smile. "I do believe that I deserve a hello kiss for this," he said, and swept her into his arms. She looked up at him, her deep blue eyes glowing.

"That's an offer I wouldn't dare refuse," she whispered, and then he was lowering his mouth to hers and she tasted so damn good. So damn delicious. Like apples and sunshine and life, all wrapped up into one. He began nibbling his way down her throat.

"You know," he murmured, swirling his tongue against the hollow of her throat where her pulse beat fast, "we could just stay here and eat each other for dinner…"

She giggled and pulled away. "No getting out of dinner that easily," she said scoldingly. "And, you better come all the way in before you let all the heat out, and the outside cats in." There was a calico cat winding its way around Declan's feet, obviously hoping for a little attention. Declan patted it on the head and then went inside, closing the door against the nippy fall air. It was going to be winter soon. There was that feel in the air that hadn't been there just days earlier.

Iris sat down in a rocking chair close to the door, her braided gold and reddish brown hair spilling in a fat braid over her shoulder. Declan handed the present over to her and then held his breath. Hopefully she loved it just as much as he thought she would. Women's clothing was always so hard to buy.

"Ohhhhh…" she breathed softly as she pulled the cashmere sweater out of the box. "Declan, it's so beautiful!"

He grinned in relief. "I thought it matched your eyes," he said proudly. The cashmere was exactly the color of her eyes when she was happy and laughing. He looked closer at her as she held it up against herself, and noticed that there were dark circles underneath those eyes. Despite the brilliance of her smile, she looked…exhausted?

Why was she exhausted?

"You doin' okay, Cookie?" he asked, kneeling down next to her. Suddenly, he felt uncomfortable looming over her while she was resting in her rocking chair. "You seem a little tired or somethin'."

"I'm fine," she said with a wave of her hand. He

stared at her doubtfully and in complete silence. Finally, she couldn't stand it any longer and blurted out, "I'm just not used to sitting all the time, is all. As an RN, I hardly ever sat while on shift. Now, that's all I do. My legs and back are tired of sitting, but I can't exactly buy a standing or a walking desk, now can I?"

"A what or a what?" he asked, confused.

"A standing desk. You stand at it. A walking desk has a treadmill that goes real slow and you walk as you work. They're both much better for you than just sitting all day." She waved her hand in the air again dismissively. "Obviously neither of those work for me. I just have to get used to it. It'll be fine. Let me go put on this sweater so we can go eat." She struggled to her feet, ignoring his offer to help her up, and strode from the room as quickly as her legs and brain injury and cane would allow her.

He sat back on his hindquarters, staring sightlessly down at Milk as she wound her way around his body, begging for some pettings. To see someone as amazing as Iris McLain get beat by something like that…

It just didn't sit right with him. Surely there had to be something they could do.

He stood up, putting his shoulders back. It was time for him to swallow his pride and ask Jennifer for help. She was busy, what with the baby and the accounting firm, but he knew she was sweet enough to want to spend the time to help him anyway, if only because she'd know how much it'd mean to Iris.

He wouldn't tell her the truth, of course, but he'd ask her for help doing searches on Google. She didn't need to know that he ran a computer just fine…as long as it was numbers he was manipulating. Excel was his friend. But he'd pretend computer stupidity if it meant getting help for his Iris.

My Iris.

He petted Milk softly as he thought about that phrase. She was his. She'd been his for years…until he'd been so stupid as to give her up.

No, he needed to be truthful with himself – he forced her away. He told her he didn't want her anymore. It was a miracle she'd agreed to go out on one date with him, let alone dozens. Let alone let him take her to bed. She shouldn't have, not really, and to think that he'd thought himself so benevolent that he'd go out on a "pity date" with her…

Well, that was one secret he'd take to the grave with him. He was pretty sure that if she knew he'd had that thought, she'd find her father's pistol and put him out of his misery. You didn't pity Iris McLain. Not if you knew what was good for you.

She came back into the living room and struck a pose. "What do you think?" she asked, holding her arm out to the side to show off the soft cashmere fabric draping over her luscious body.

My Iris indeed. As long as I don't screw this up.

CHAPTER 22

IRIS

*S*HE EASED INTO the kitchen chair, trying to stretch out the muscles in her legs and jiggle some life back into them. It was break time from coding, and she needed to do something that didn't involve a computer screen. Which meant, of course, that she was working on a cane.

She picked up the long piece of pine that her dad had brought back from his last hunt; he'd gone out for an elk hunt but had picked up some branches for her, too. After curing and straightening them for her, it was then up to her to make something beautiful out of them.

This particular stick was turning out exceptionally well, with the pattern of the wood showing through nicely. The warm honey glow of the pine made it feel like a warm lap blanket you could snuggle down with…a lap blanket that happened to be made out of pine, of course.

She looked up from her carving to peer out the kitchen window into the white expanse outside. Winter had hit, and with a vengeance. It'd been snowing most of the day, which was both so peaceful to watch as the snowflakes slowly drifted down, and depressing as hell.

Because this meant that it would be the big sledding party over at the Miller's house today. Her eyes flicked to her phone and then back out the window again. It was white and peaceful and beautiful as far as the eye could see. The old Iris, the six-months-ago Iris, would've been throwing on snow pants and boots, going outside into the white world with her sled, heading over to the Miller place so she could join the throngs of people enjoying the best sledding hill in the county.

The Iris of six months ago was damn spoiled, and hadn't even realized it.

Her willpower broke, and she snatched up her phone, opening the Facebook app and scrolling through for the event invitation. Sure enough, on the Long Valley Facebook page, Jennifer had posted an open invitation to anyone in Long Valley to come sled in their backyard. Iris hadn't been home for one of the Miller sledding parties in years, but she could still remember how amazing Carmelita's hot cocoa was, and how much fun that hill was.

She closed her eyes, ignoring the hot prick of... water in her eyes. They were just tired from trying to concentrate on a computer screen for hours on end.

And anyway, what was she thinking, looking at her phone while on her break? The whole point of her break was not to look at a computer. She couldn't give into temptation like that again. She had to just keep going. No point in looking back.

No point in wishing for what she couldn't have. She turned back to the walking-stick-in-the-making in front of her. She could make beautiful canes and walking sticks. This was something she could do. And she loved doing it.

And that would just have to be good enough.

She swallowed hard.

Ugh.

Things she loved…like Declan Miller.

Even now, after a month and a half of being with him (this time around, anyway), she couldn't understand what he saw in her. Didn't he look at her and wish for his old Iris back? Didn't he wonder what life could've been like, if she hadn't been so tired one night?

And what did he think was going to happen? Where was their relationship going? She'd still never gathered up the courage to force him to tell her why he'd broken up with her to begin with. The real reason. She didn't believe, not for one second, that he suddenly felt a burning desire to attend the U of I because they had a better ag program. That was total bullshit, and she knew it.

But even if she somehow found her backbone at some point (and a large part of her knew she needed to, and pronto) and the reason he gave was rational (although she couldn't begin to guess what a rational reason could be, and she'd had a lot of years to spend guessing) they still couldn't get married. He couldn't marry Iris. Maybe he just hadn't thought about it. Maybe this was just some sort of fun fling until he found someone he could really marry and have kids with.

Because God only knew, she wasn't that person. She couldn't climb into his pickup truck without him helping her in, and every time he did, she was still afraid she was going to fall on her head and get a second brain injury on the console.

And that was just his truck! She couldn't grow a garden. She couldn't can green beans. She couldn't go help him stack hay bales in preparation for winter. She couldn't even bake cookies without practically setting the house on fire.

She couldn't be a farmer's wife. And someday, Declan was going to wise up and figure that out.

And she was gonna be in a world of hurt when he did.

And yet somehow, she couldn't make herself break up with him. Even though she knew, absolutely knew without a doubt, that it'd be the smart thing to do.

For someone who prided herself on being intelligent, she sure was acting dumb.

CHAPTER 23

DECLAN

He pulled up to Iris' house, his stomach in knots. He hadn't been this nervous since he'd first asked Iris out on a date all those weeks ago. Their pity date. He rolled his eyes at himself. How dumb he'd been back then.

But now…he had something he really thought Iris would love. It was going to be awesome. He was excited and nervous and happy and wound up tighter than an eight-day clock. If he knew his Iris – and he really thought he did – she was going to love this. Then, after he surprised her with the present, they could have a nice evening of watching movies and eating popcorn and snuggling on the couch.

Yup, tonight was gonna be a great night.

He grabbed the present off the passenger-side seat, this time wrapped by Jennifer. She'd helped him with this project, for which he was eternally grateful.

If he'd been stuck on his own trying to figure it out... well, he wouldn't have, plain and simple.

One of the outside cats came winding over, rubbing up against Declan's legs, and he leaned down and petted it for a moment. For being an outside cat, it was in pretty good shape. The extra calories from Iris' feedings must be helping.

He crunched through the snow, the package tucked under his arm. He raised his hand to knock on the door when it flew open and Iris sent him a huge grin. "Hey, darlin'," she said, kissing him as he passed her and into the house. Dropping the package into her rocking chair, he pulled her up against the closed front door and snuggled her between his thighs.

He looked down at her and smiled. "Hi there, Cookie," he breathed, and then took his sweet time kissing her. She tasted like chocolate and coffee, and when he pulled back, he asked her teasingly, "Enjoying your new chocolate-flavored coffee creamer?"

"You know it," she said with a laugh. "You know, you really should stop buying me presents. I'm going to get spoiled."

"Well, that's just the way I like my girls." He held his breath, wondering if she'd object to the term "my girls" but she didn't bat an eyelash, instead sinking into the rocking chair and tugging on the gold, shimmery ribbon enclosing the package.

"It's heavy," she said absentmindedly, biting her

lower lip in concentration as she worked to undo the wrapping.

"Thankfully the online store had free shipping, or it would've cost an arm and a leg to get it here," he admitted cheerfully. In his humble opinion, online shopping was one of the best things to hit small rural communities. No more driving 90 minutes to Boise to buy obscure items.

And this was definitely an obscure item.

She pulled the box out and stared at it for a moment in bewilderment. "Hovr?" she asked. She tilted her head to the side, trying to figure out what she was holding. "What is this?" she finally asked, giving up and looking up at him.

"Jennifer helped me find it," he said, pulling the strap and metal out of the box. "See this strap? It connects to the bottom side of your desk. It hangs down," he held the strap up in the air to demonstrate, "and this metal bar with round pads on it? You put your feet on the pads and you can move them around. Basically, you're walking without ever standing up from your desk!"

Horrifyingly, she burst into tears and threw herself into his arms. He patted her back awkwardly. *Oh God, oh God, what do I do?*

"I didn't mean to upset you!" he said, patting her back furiously. Oreo was head-butting her leg, obviously upset that she was upset. "You said that you're struggling with sitting all the time, and I thought this way, you could be sitting, but still moving. We first found those walking desks you'd talked about, but obviously that wasn't going to work, and then we found this and we thought it'd be great and…please don't cry!"

He was just contemplating getting down on his hands and knees and begging her to stop crying when she lifted her tear-stained face and looked at him.

"These are happy tears," she informed him, laughing as she said it. She quickly sobered back up and said softly, "I can't believe you did this – that you found this. Declan, it means so much to me."

He leaned over and kissed her again, just lightly this time, and then wiped her tears away with the pads of his thumbs. "You know, you could warn a guy sometime that you're spilling happy tears," he grumped, but he couldn't pretend to be upset for long. Her dazzling smile wouldn't let him.

"C'mon," she said, pulling away a little and tugging at his hand. "Are you going to install it for me?" But she must've moved too quickly without thinking about it, because she toppled over…and landed face first against his groin.

He had to admit, if only to himself, that this had to be the first time that her screwy balance was 100% a wonderful thing, in his humble opinion.

She pushed herself back up, breathless and red in the face. He was happy to note that her face quite brilliantly matched her hair.

All thoughts of installing the Hovr, of watching a

movie or snuggling with Iris on the couch, flew right out of his head. Impulsively, he scooped her up in his arms and carried her to her bedroom.

It was time to show Iris McLain just how much he loved her.

CHAPTER 24

IRIS

*O*NCE HE'D CARRIED HER into her bedroom, he let her slide down the front of him, slowly, achingly, torturously. She could feel him, his erection straining against his jeans, and she grinned to herself. She'd never cop to it out loud, of course, but she had to admit that at least this one time, losing her balance had worked out quite nicely. If she'd known what Declan's reaction was going to be, she might've managed to "accidentally" fall over onto his groin before now.

Well, better late than never.

She leaned in towards him and he mirrored her movements, obviously expecting a kiss. In a cheeky mood, though, Iris intentionally avoided his lips and instead landed her kiss on the side of his neck, just below his jawline. Declan chuckled and then immediately tilted his head to the side, opening his neck up further to her affections. He was obviously happy to receive kisses, no matter where they landed.

As she worked along his jawline with her lips and tongue, her hands worked equally hard to release the buttons of his shirt. One by one, the dastardly enclosures keeping him encased in his shirt popped free. She continued her kissing exploration as she tugged his shirt out of his Wranglers, and then worked her way over to the small dip at the base of his throat formed by his collarbone, as she pulled the sleeves of his shirt down his thick arms.

"You like your girls spoiled," she breathed, finally pulling her lips far enough away from his warm skin to speak. "Well, I like my boys equally as spoiled."

Declan chuckled at her words as she resumed her downward progression of kisses. Her lips surrounded one of his flat nipples and she drew the sensitive flesh lightly into her mouth, letting her tongue play over the hardened bump, much like he loved to do to her. She heard him suck in a sharp breath and mentally patted herself on the back. It may've been years, but she still remembered how sensitive his nipples were.

"I think…I…could stand…to be spoiled…a little…" he managed to say, his breath short and ragged.

She moved downward, kissing along his bare chest. She slipped her fingers behind his belt, using the broad leather strap for support as she lowered herself uncertainly to her knees. She held tight to him for a moment, making sure she could support herself in the position she hadn't been in since her accident.

When she managed to stay upright without feeling even a little tipsy, she felt pride spread through her veins. She really was getting better.

She continued to lay kisses on his skin, moving along the line of denim formed by his jeans, as her hands made quick work of his belt and then the fly.

Just as the top button slipped out, releasing the tension of the fabric, she felt his hand come to rest on top of her head. For just a moment, her body tensed at the touch, but she quickly realized that he wasn't directing or forcing her, but instead was simply excited. Her shoulders relaxed and she felt a thrill run through her at the idea that despite all that was wrong with her body, he still wanted her.

Her lips explored lower, following the new v-shaped line of his open fly as she dug her fingers into his muscular ass. She groaned appreciatively against his skin; she didn't know what he did to stay in such good shape, but whatever it was, she was in heaven.

As she shoved his pants and underwear down to the floor, she noticed a distinct tan line that followed the waist of his jeans. She paused her kissing of his skin for a moment to appreciate the contrast between the golden brown of his tanned chest, and his white hips. Thoughts of him standing bare-chested in the middle of a field on a warm summer day flooded her mind, and body. She giggled mischievously at the sexy thought. There was a sight she wouldn't grow tired of…

"What are you laughing at?" Declan asked, amusement apparent in his voice.

"I'm just thinking about you standing bare-chested in an open field," Iris responded, wrapping her hand around his rigid shaft as she spoke.

"It's a bit cold for that right now, but next summer you're welcome to come out to the field anytime," he responded, while running his fingers through her hair and his voice taking on an equally mischievous tone. "Show up at the right time and I may not be the only one in the field without a shirt on."

She grinned at the naughty thought before she returned her attention to stroking him, while her mind automatically listed out all the things she found wonderfully endearing about this man, including the fact that he could laugh with her even during the most intimate of moments. She lifted his length upward and ran her tongue up the underside of him, feeling her own excitement grow in time with his.

Declan groaned and his dick hardened even further in her mouth, chasing away any feelings of trepidation she'd had. It'd been years since she'd done anything like this and she was wary of screwing things up, but based on how often he flexed his fingers around the back of her head in encouragement, she was pretty sure she was doing it right.

She was caught up in her own mental reverie when Declan surprised her. He pulled out of her mouth and, reaching down, placed his hands under her arms and helped her to a standing position. She looked at him, confused. She knew he'd been enjoying what she'd been doing, so why…

"I've thought about this, a lot," he said in a husky voice before kissing her. The kiss was rough and full of desire, as he buried his hands deep into her hair. When they finally came up for air, he whispered, "There's a way I've wanted to take you for a very long time. I thought about it when we were teenagers and now…I can't get the thought out of my mind."

Iris was both curious as well as worried. The reality was, she might not be capable of some of the more…acrobatic positions a couple could use in bed.

But Declan didn't wait for her response, or for her to worry her way out of it. Placing his hands on her hips, he swung her around so she was facing toward the bed. Her legs began to shake with excitement, which just increased the worry she was feeling. If she couldn't even stand properly, she probably couldn't do…whatever it was he had in mind.

Before she could say anything, though, Declan's strong arms wrapped around her, and his large body pressed up against her back, silently begging for her to lean into him. She held herself stiff for a moment, the worry almost causing her to panic, but with a whoosh, she made herself relax and trust him completely. He held still, not moving an inch, until she leaned into him, letting her choose when it was time to move forward.

When she did, she felt his breath quicken, and then he whispered, "Thank you."

Thank you for trusting me.

She nodded once, not relying on her voice to speak. She could've said the same thing – *thank you for wanting me, even though I am broken. Thank you for your patience. Thank you for your love.*

But she said nothing at all, just letting her body speak for her.

With impressive quickness, Declan worked the hooks, buttons, and buckles of her clothing until their naked bodies pressed together. His soft lips pressed kisses on the back of her neck as he ran his hands up and down the front of her body, his fingers bumping slowly and provocatively over her hardening nipples. The entire time he explored her, he kept his arms wrapped around her body, holding her up, and never once did she question his support.

She knew she could rely on him fully, and that was the most freeing feeling of all.

After a long and…thorough inspection of every nook and cranny of her body, Declan placed a hand on her upper back, encouraging her to bend over at the waist. She felt a flash of doubt but quickly squashed it, reminding herself that she'd promised to rely on him completely.

With a deep breath, she placed her hands on the mattress and spread her feet apart slightly, relying on the bed to help her keep her balance.

Declan held her hips firmly, and then she felt his

tip, seeking her out. She spread her feet just a little bit more, the need for him to be inside her overwhelming. Declan found her center and with a slow, fluid push, he entered her.

Once he was fully inside, he moved his hands, reaching his burly forearm completely around her tiny waist, holding her to him, as he began to ease in and out of her. The granite surety of him erased any residual worry she had about falling.

Finally, she let herself completely succumb to the incredible physical sensations, as well as the pure relief that came from relinquishing her personal worries.

For just a little while, she was just Iris, and he was just Declan, and together, they were just happy. Blissfully, completely, wonderfully happy.

CHAPTER 25

IRIS

*I*RIS LEANED against the kitchen sink, using it to stabilize herself, as she scrubbed the red potatoes piled up in its ceramic depths. They'd hired the local catering company – Belly Bliss Catering – to provide most of the food, tables, and chairs for the party, but her mom requested the McLain Red Potato Salad, which could only be made if the person knew the secret recipe for it. Being a McLain daughter, Iris had of course been taught the recipe many years ago, and she figured it was only fair to make it in honor of her parents' 40th wedding anniversary.

Caterers and staff members bustled in and out of the house, the door slamming closed behind them every time they went, but Iris ignored it all. It was about two weeks until Christmas, and the scene outside her parents' kitchen window was simply gorgeous, if a little disconcerting. Her own MIL apartment was attached to the backside of her parents' house, so the views outside were to the same general scenery, although shifted just slightly to the left. It was like looking out her kitchen window, but seeing everything a bit out of place.

The house wasn't big enough to hold everyone and the Sawyer Community Center was booked up, so Iris and Ivy had arranged for two large white tents with propane burners to be set up in the yard instead. They also had a large bonfire set up and ready to go in the middle. Iris figured between it all, people would probably be able to stay warm, if they were smart and were bundled up too.

Ivy came into the house, muttering darkly. "Iris!" she yelped as soon as she saw her. She tossed her curly red hair back over her shoulder. Iris had to admit, even if only to herself, that she was jealous of the curls. Her own hair was straight as an arrow. "You would *not* believe who is here!" Ivy continued, stalking over to the counter and grabbing an apple slice from the caterer's tray. She began munching on it noisily.

Iris grabbed another potato and gave it a light scrub. "Yeah?" she prompted. Ivy tended to be a bit dramatic, so she wasn't surprised that she'd gotten so angry over a guest already. Hell, the party was just getting started, but that was Ivy for you.

"Tiffany and Ezzy! You didn't invite them, did you?"

Iris stopped scrubbing the potatoes for a moment and turned to glare at her sister. Ivy shrunk back. "I didn't think so, I just thought I'd ask," she mumbled sheepishly.

Iris rolled her eyes, and didn't even bother answering. If Ivy sincerely thought that her one and only sister, one of her closest friends in all the world, could intentionally invite two girls to a party who'd made her life miserable all the way through high school...well, Iris had no words to say to her.

None that she should be uttering at her parents' house in the middle of a party, anyway.

When the silence extended out into painful territory, finally Ivy mumbled, "I'm sorry. I shouldn't have said that."

Iris jerked her head once in response, and with that, the little tiff was over. She began gathering the cleaned potatoes to move them over to the kitchen table so she could sit while chopping them. Her legs were already getting tired, and her eyes were aching from trying to keep everything lined up the way they should be. It was never good when the world tilted suddenly without warning.

Well, she shouldn't say never. There was that time she'd fallen face first into Declan's lap...

She cleared her throat, forcing her mind to focus on the present, and began juggling the cutting board and her cane, trying to get everything she needed to the kitchen table. She really should've had this salad done hours ago, but when the caterers had shown up, Iris had quickly realized that someone had to take charge or nothing would ever get done. All plans of getting the salad finished before guests showed up flew out the window.

"My best guess," Iris mused aloud as she slowly moved items over to the table, "is that they heard about the free food and music, and decided to come on down and mooch off us. They're the kinds of people who would think that'd be okay."

Ivy considered that for a moment and then sighed. "You're right." She grabbed the last item – a bowl of washed potatoes – and carried them over to the table for her. Iris smiled up in gratitude at her younger sister. She may be impulsive and say stupid things sometimes, but she could also be sweet and thoughtful. It was one of the reasons she hadn't killed her yet.

"Thanks, sis," she said, drawing the bowl towards her and pulling out potatoes.

"Well, they've ruined everything," Ivy announced dramatically, crunching her way through another apple slice. Iris was pretty sure the caterers would kill her when they saw what Ivy was doing to their beautifully constructed fruit platter, but Iris also figured she'd let the caterers do the killing. Sometimes, it was just easier.

"Everything?" Iris echoed. That seemed a bit… over the top.

"Yeah! There was this guy, and—"

"Hey, you guys, I need to know where you want this table," one of the caterers said, popping his head around the kitchen door.

Iris started to struggle to her feet, but Ivy waved her off. "You sit and take a break and get the damn salad done already. There are rumblings in the ranks that no one has brought the famous McLain salad out yet. I'll go." She snagged another apple slice and headed out the door, their voices cut off as the kitchen door thunked closed behind them.

A guy... Iris wondered what that was all about. She'd seen Ivy talking to Austin earlier, although she'd only been watching them through the kitchen window, and thus couldn't hear what was being said. Ivy had almost looked like she was...flirting with Austin, which just couldn't be right. Ivy didn't do cowboys *or* extension agents, which just happened to be what Austin was.

Well, that and one of Declan's closest friends.

Austin wasn't from around there — he grew up in the panhandle — but apparently him and Dec had met when Declan had broken up with her and moved up north to the U of I to get his bachelor's degree.

Although Iris tried her hardest not to think about that time in their lives — it was damn depressing, if she let herself think about it too much — she did have to admit that Austin was one good result out of the whole thing. The three of them had hung out a few times, and Iris had found the soft-spoken cowboy to be a real gentleman. Declan had invited him to move to Long Valley, apparently, when the previous extension agent had retired, and Austin had been in town ever since.

Well, whether that was the guy in question or not, Ivy wasn't going to be happy once she figured out who he was. She lived in California and was comfortable there. Honestly, she was a snot when it came to small towns located in Idaho, and even worse when it came to cowboys who lived in small towns located in Idaho.

Iris was surprised Austin had managed to get Ivy to even talk to him.

"Hey, Cookie," Declan's deep voice rumbled behind her, just as he dropped a kiss on the crown of her head.

"Oh hi!" she said, jumping about five feet in the air. Okay, not really that far – she couldn't jump that high even before her accident – but plenty high enough in her estimation. He laughed down at her as she panted, her hand over her heart.

"I really shouldn't sneak up on you when you have a knife in your hand," he said dryly. "I'm thinking major damage could happen that way."

She stuck her tongue out at him, not willing to admit he was right. "Humph," she grumbled, which was as good of a come back as she could come up with.

And even she admitted that it wasn't very good.

"You almost done? There are a lot of guests out there." He stood behind her and rubbed her shoulders as she continued to chop her way through the potatoes.

"I wish," she groused. "It'll be a while. You should go out there and mingle, though. I'll be along as soon as I'm done." Although, his hands on her shoulders did feel heavenly…

He moved away, and she sighed.

"All right, if you insist," he said. "I don't want you to feel abandoned, all alone in the kitchen."

"Oh, I'm not alone," she said, waving her knife around in the air breezily. "The caterers come in quite regularly."

Declan laughed. "All right," he said, dropping a kiss on top of her head again. "I'll see you outside when you're done?"

"Sounds good."

She watched him walk out the door, the easy sway of his hips almost hypnotic. Damn, he was a good-looking guy. And for some reason unbeknownst to her, he didn't seem to mind that she was a cripple.

She figured life just didn't get any better than that.

CHAPTER 26

DECLAN

*D*ECLAN STOOD next to Mr. Burgemeister as they chatted about beef prices and what everyone expected to happen to them this spring – drop, of course; no group of people on earth were as negatively optimistic as a group of ranchers and farmers – when the song *The Dance* by Garth Brooks came on. Declan paused, memories washing over him.

It was their high school senior prom. Iris was smiling up at him in her shimmery gold dress as he escorted her out onto the dance floor. She'd been so gorgeous that night, with her curled hair up in pins, and a dress that showed off all her curves…he hadn't been able to breathe as he held her in his arms and they swayed to the haunting notes.

He'd known then that he'd always love her. And as dumb as he'd been as a teenage boy – and hormones made him do some pretty damn dumb things at times – he'd been right about that.

Declan waited for Mr. Burgemeister to finish his rant on skyrocketing feed prices and then quickly slipped in, "I think this is my cue – I'm going to go find my girlfriend and ask her for a dance."

Mr. Burgemeister paused for a moment, thrown off his stride, and then his eyes began to twinkle. "If I had a choice between a beautiful young lady or a blustering old fool like me, I'd pick her, too. Good luck, son."

"Thanks." Declan tipped his hat and then set off across to the tent where Iris was standing with Ivy and Abby, chatting about…something. He snuck up behind her and wrapped his arms around her slender waist, whispering, "Will you dance with me?" in her ear.

Instead of melting back against him like he'd expected, though, she stiffened in his arms and slowly maneuvered around to face him. "Declan, you know I can't dance," she said in a sharp, frustrated voice, holding up her cane as evidence. "I—"

"I can hold you up," he interrupted, his brow wrinkling in confusion.

"Don't make me feel bad," Iris replied, a frown crossing her face. "I already feel awful because I'm practically a cripple. Please don't throw this in my face."

He jerked back, his spine straight as a measuring stick. *What the hell? That isn't what I meant at all.*

"I wasn't throwing it in your face," he said slowly, the pain and anger at her words bleeding through his voice, despite his best efforts to keep it neutral. "You should rely on me to hold you up. Why can't you trust me to be there for you?"

She stared up at him, anger setting her mouth into a firm slash across her face. "Declan, it isn't always about you. I'm the one who can't walk, not you. I know my limits. Dancing isn't on the agenda, now or ever. Period, end of story. If you're going to be in my life, you need to know this and not just ignore reality because it doesn't suit you."

"Doesn't suit me?" he repeated, thrown off by her words. "I've been trying really hard to accommodate—"

"Thanks for coming out this cold wintry afternoon to help us celebrate Betty and John McLain's 40th wedding anniversary!" Ivy's voice cut through their escalating argument as she shouted to the group as a whole. Iris turned her back on Declan pointedly, facing her sister to listen to her talk. With a sigh, Declan turned too.

He wasn't quite sure how a desire to slow dance with the love of his life had somehow turned into an argument in front of the entire population of Long Valley, but dammit all, it had. Just when he thought he had Iris figured out, she turned everything on its head again.

CHAPTER 27

IRIS

*I*RIS SMILED AND NODDED and clapped politely as Ivy gave her spontaneous welcoming speech to the crowd of well-wishers, but inside, she was seething. Just a few hours earlier, she'd been so happy as she'd sat in the kitchen, making the potato salad and contemplating how wonderful it was that Declan didn't seem to notice or care that she was a cripple.

Well, she was starting to realize that there was a downside to that optimistic positivity that Declan brought to every situation. He had to understand that she wasn't like everyone else. She couldn't do all that he wanted.

Or all that she wanted.

She deflated a little, her shoulders sagging. Dammit all. As much as she hated to admit the truth, her biggest frustration wasn't with Declan and his inability to realize how crippled she really was.

It was with herself. It was so damn frustrating and angering and terrifying and awful and horrific that she couldn't just go out there and dance with her boyfriend. It used to be one of their favorite pastimes, and now...now she couldn't do it.

And she hated that.

And she took that out on Declan.

As another member in the community who Iris didn't recognize stood up and rambled on about how much her parents meant to him, Iris realized she needed to apologize to Declan, even if now wasn't exactly the time to talk through things. She could verbally apologize to him later. For now...

She moved back slightly, pressing her body against Declan's. She heard a hiss of indrawn breath as he jerked just slightly in surprise. She nestled up against him and tilted her head back. "Sorry," she mouthed. He grinned down at her and wrapped his arms around her, tucking her head underneath his chin and holding her close as they listened to the speeches.

She sighed happily. They still needed to have that discussion, and Declan still needed to know that there truly were limits on her body, but for now? This would do.

Finally, the speechmaking ended and the crowd broke up, heading back to the tables for more food or over to the propane heaters to warm up. Declan asked softly in her ear, "Are you ready to sit down?" She nodded. Today had been more physically draining than any day since her accident, what with cooking in the kitchen and then standing outside as she talked to people. Her legs were tired, and her eyes even more so.

He guided her over to a camp chair and after settling her in, he trotted down to her house and brought back the soft blanket she always kept draped over the back of her couch.

"Thank you," she said humbly, as he tucked the blanket into place. Close to a heater and the blanket wrapped around her, she was toasty warm and quite happy.

Declan looked around and said bemusedly, "Well, that wasn't well thought out, was it. I forgot to snag a chair for me, too. Let me go hunt one down so I can sit next to you."

"Oh, you don't have to," Iris protested. "If you want to wander around and mingle, I'm quite happy to just hang out here."

"Eh, I see enough of these old farts—" he winked at her, "—down at Frank's Feed. Let me go find something to plant my ass in. I'll be right back."

Iris snuggled back into her chair with a stupidly happy grin on her face, and looked around at the party in progress. There was her mom, talking to Mrs. Burgemeister about canning recipes for pickles, and she could just spot her dad, chewing the fat with Mr. Frank, the owner of Frank's Feed & Fuel.

Everyone's faces were red from the cold, but the adorable knitted hats and scarves that the women were sporting made Iris wish they held outdoor parties all the time, especially in the dead of winter. If even she could manage the cold and the ice and the snow, then really, no one else had an excuse, at least as far as she figured it.

She glanced over and saw Declan chatting with his brother Stetson, who was bouncing Flint on his shoulder, a baby blanket thrown over it to protect his shirt from any potential spit-up Flint might fling his way.

What a sight to see – Stetson with his own baby. She remembered back to high school, when he'd still been in elementary and such a baby himself. A cute baby, but one nonetheless. To look at him now, she could almost forget what he looked like with one front tooth missing and his hair standing straight up in the back in a permanent cowlick.

Seeing him grown-up and married, a child of his own…well, it made her feel older than dirt, really. Sure, she was only 35, but she felt about a thousand years old, and that was before she really spent much time thinking about how grown up Stetson was.

Declan and Stetson laughed together, and then Stetson asked teasingly, his voice floating on the slight breeze, "So when are you gonna get yourself one of these little buggers?" He patted Flint on the back, his small body looking even smaller beneath Stetson's large hands.

Iris froze.

CHAPTER 28

DECLAN

He left his gorgeous Iris in search of an unoccupied camp chair. He needed to show her that he was willing to fit into her life, which meant sitting next to her and hanging out with her, not wandering off and leaving her alone, no matter what she said she was okay with.

He'd been chewing over their little spat before the speeches had begun, and best as he could figure, she didn't seem to trust that he'd take care of her. She seemed to think that she had to do everything on her own, without relying on him for anything, including holding her up while they danced.

Come hell or high water, he was determined to show her that wasn't true. No matter what, he was going to take care of her. He loved her too damn much not to.

"Hey, brother," Stetson said, interrupting Declan's thoughts, and his search for a chair. His younger brother was holding Flint, his beautiful baby boy. He was swaddled up so well in coats and boots and scarves and hats and mittens, Declan could barely spot his tiny eyes peering out at the world.

"You're brave, taking a kid like this out into the cold," Declan said. He reached out and stroked Flint over his knitted cap, the flaps tied securely over his tiny ears. It was hard to fathom that he'd ever been this small, although the baby pictures his mom used to show him attested otherwise.

But Flint was just so little.

"Eh, Jennifer put so many layers on him, I think he could survive a trip to Antartica at this point," Stetson said with a laugh. "So when are you gonna get yourself one of these little buggers?" He patted Flint on the back soothingly as the little guy started to squirm. He quickly fell back into his papa's arms, content to just hang out for the moment.

Declan looked at his nephew as love swelled up inside of him. "Damn, I don't know. If I could know for sure that my kid would take after Iris instead of me in the looks department, well then, maybe I'd be willing to give it a try. You wouldn't want this ugly mug on a kid, though." He stroked his chin and stared off into the distance for a moment, striking a pose for Stetson. He enjoyed the hearty chuckle that Stetson let loose, and decided that he ought to flip some shit at him, as any good older brother would do.

"It's obvious that you got lucky with this one," he said, patting Flint on the back. "He's the spittin' image of Jennifer. Can you imagine if he'd looked a damn thing like you?" Stetson let out a roar of laughter.

Actually, the kid was cute as a button and he looked just like Stetson had as a baby, but what kind of an older brother would he be if he said something like that? They'd probably take his Older Brother Card away from him. A body couldn't just go around, complimenting his siblings. That was crazy talk.

As he looked into Flint's sleepy eyes, though, slowly settling closed and then jerking back open as he struggled to stay awake just one minute more, Declan realized that despite his teasing, having a kid was absolutely what he wanted.

Having a kid with Iris was all that he wanted.

He sobered up and said seriously, "I do want a baby, though. Ten of 'em, if Iris will let me."

Stetson let out a choked laugh. "You might want to start with one and go from there," he said dryly.

Declan waved his comment away. "I'll take as many as she'll give me. Speaking of, I was supposed to be rustlin' up a chair so I could sit next to her. I better get a move on."

"I saw a free chair over there," Stetson said, pointing past the food tables, "about ten minutes ago. No idea if it's still free or not, though."

Declan nodded his thanks and headed that direction. He walked past the large bonfire, roaring and shooting up sparks into the quickly deepening twilight, and felt a twist of joy and pleasure shoot through him at the sight. He ought to move Iris over to the bonfire. She'd enjoy the large flames and everyone standing around it, chatting and singing Christmas carols.

He finally spotted a lonely camp chair, abandoned in the shadows cast by the dancing flames, and headed towards it quickly. He wanted to snag it before someone else realized it was free. Iris was probably wondering where on earth he'd gone. This had taken a lot longer than he'd anticipated. Finding a free chair was harder—

"Hey," Abby said as she tapped him on the shoulder. He spun on the icy snow, surprised by her sudden appearance.

"Oh my God, Abby, you gave me a heart attack," he said, laughing. But her face was stone-cold serious as she looked back at him, and he quickly sobered up. "What's wrong?" he asked, panic beginning to wind its way through his veins.

"You need to take Iris home," she said in a clipped tone of voice, jerking her head back towards where he'd left her. He couldn't see her through the crowds and the bonfire and the gathering darkness, but whatever was going on, Abby seemed to think it was something awful. Her normally happy, open face was drawn into a deep scowl.

One that seemed to be directed straight at him.

"What's going on?" he asked, flummoxed. He'd never had his sister-in-law even slightly unhappy with him, let alone pissed.

He couldn't begin to guess what was going on.

"Go take care of her," Abby ordered, and Declan could suddenly see how she'd made it as a police officer all these years. An angry Abby wasn't someone he wanted to mess around with.

He jerked his head in acknowledgment and took off with a brisk trot. Whatever it was, he'd fix it. Had he been gone too long? Iris had said that she was fine being left by herself, but maybe she hadn't really meant it. Girls did that sometimes – they'd say one thing but expect you to know that they really felt something else completely different. Maybe she'd gone and pulled that stunt on him.

But when he could finally see Iris, he realized something else was wrong. Really wrong. His prideful, stubborn, independent, smart, amazing Iris…was crying.

In public.

In all the years he'd known her, he'd only known her to shed happy tears. She'd never cried from pain or sadness or anger, even that time she broke her leg while they were out hiking in high school.

But even in the awful lighting being cast from the bonfire and propane burners, he could tell that these were not happy tears.

Had someone said something to her? Made fun of her? He felt anger boiling up inside of him at whoever'd made her feel like this. He'd find them and beat them and make them wish they'd never been such assholes. He'd make them pay. No one made his Iris feel awful.

No one.

But when he got to her side and dropped to his knees, she just looked at him, eyes dead. Blank. There was no love, no happiness, no joy. "I'd like to go home now," she said firmly, in complete contrast to the tears rolling down her face.

"Of course," he said, helping her to her feet and draping the blanket over his arm. "Are you okay? What happened?"

She didn't answer but instead snuffled once or twice, dashed the tears away on her cheeks and shoved her arm through his, using him to help her balance on the tricky icy ground. Using her cane for balance, they walked slowly through the gathering. They wished goodnight to anyone who talked to them, but never stopped moving, slowly, painfully, through the throngs and over to her MIL apartment. He helped her down the two front steps to the sunken front door, and opened it for her. She walked through…and slammed the door in his face.

He stared at the closed door in front of him for a long minute.

Yup, that had just happened, and he had *no* idea why.

CHAPTER 29

IRIS

*I*RIS SHUFFLED OVER TO HER COUCH, threw her cane down next to it, and dropped into it with a howl of tears.

How could Declan be so smart and thoughtful... and completely stupid at the same time?

Ten kids?

Ten kids?!

Who the hell was he kidding? She couldn't handle one kid. What if she lost her balance and tipped over while carrying their child? Babies didn't have fully formed, hard skulls to protect their brains until they were 18 months old. She could give a child brain damage because of her godawful balance. She wasn't fit to be a mother to a guinea pig, let alone a child.

Let alone ten children.

Oreo nudged her arm and then licked his way up it, obviously upset that she was upset. She reached out her arm and pulled him up against her, snuggling her face against his soft fur. His purrs vibrated through her body as she wet him with her tears. "I probably shouldn't even have you two," she said softly, although her heart twisted at the thought of it. She couldn't let her cats go. She'd just have to be careful not to pick them up when she was tired. Or walking at all, for that matter.

She groaned through her tears, and Oreo upped his purr, practically vibrating his way off the couch in an attempt to comfort her.

"I was stupid, Oreo," she said into his fur, so softly that the words were coming out as breathy whispers instead of formed words. "Twice in one day, Declan proved to me that he just doesn't know what I'm really like. What my disabilities really are. This is my fault, of course – I've tried so damn hard to hide them from him. I don't want someone to look at me and see my disabilities, especially him. I want him to see *me*.

"But I think…" Her voice trembled with pain at the words she was about to say; painful to even think, but oh-so-true. "I think Declan's been okay with dating me because he doesn't realize that I'm disabled. He's somehow convinced himself that I'm just like every other girl out there. Once he realizes just how much work I am, just how little I can really trust my body…he won't want me anymore.

"I have to break things off with him before it gets to that point. I can't keep pretending that I'm fine, because I'm not. I'm not…"

She drifted off to sleep on the couch, exhausted

from her long day of frustration at the world, at Declan, and most importantly, at herself. Oreo stayed curled up in her arms, not moving an inch, as she drifted into a dreamless, boneless sleep.

The next morning, she awoke with a jerk, startling Oreo and Milk, who jumped off the couch, the night's snuggling apparently finished. Iris looked around her living room bleary-eyed, trying to figure out where she was at and what she was doing there. Why was she on the couch instead of in bed? And why did her eyes ache so much?

Then last night came rushing over her and she lay back on the couch with a groan. She'd made a fool out of herself. She'd left her parents' 40th wedding anniversary party without saying goodbye to them or helping with cleanup, and she'd cried in public.

As far as she figured it, there really wasn't anything else she could've done that would've made the evening before even more embarrassing, except maybe strip down naked and go running through the party while singing the lyrics to *It's My Party and I'll Cry if I Want To*.

Even she had to admit that that scenario would mean even more embarrassment.

But only just slightly.

She looked out of the living room windows and saw that a thick layer of fresh snow had fallen overnight. Hopefully the storm had hit after everyone had gone home for the evening. Either way, she ought to help shovel it up, even if she only did her front steps. She could hold a shovel with one hand and her cane with the other.

She forced herself off the couch and, grabbing her cane, made her way to the bedroom. She would change into her snow pants and jacket and bundle up against the cold before she went out. As long as she was careful, she could take care of her own home. It was the least she could do.

She struggled into her clothes and boots, and then grabbed her snow shovel from the hall closet where her parents had stashed it when they'd moved her in. She paused, holding the handle, and then slowly put it back, grabbing her outside broom instead. It would be better to use it. She could sweep the snow off the front steps, and feed the outside cats while she was at it.

Pleased with her new plan, she closed the coat closet and opened up the front door. A wall of cold air hit her and seared her lungs. Wow, it'd gotten cold overnight. She was thankful it hadn't been these temperatures yesterday; the party wouldn't have been nearly as much fun if it'd been sub-zero, even with propane burners and the bonfire.

She closed the front door behind her, and then, leaning on her cane, shuffled over to the bottom step leading up to the driveway beyond. Slowly, painstakingly, she brushed off one whole step. Leaning on her cane heavily, she rested for a moment. She was so damn sick of being this pathetically weak.

C'mon, Iris, get a move on.

She forced her body up to the second step and began sweeping. Just a little longer, and she could go back inside, into the warmth. She shifted her cane, trying to maneuver out of the way of the broom, when the world tilted on her and she began falling.

Arms windmilling, the concrete rushed up to greet her, and then all was black.

CHAPTER 30

DECLAN

*D*ECLAN PACED in front of Iris' dark apartment. There was no answer. He'd knocked three times, each time louder and more emphatic.

Nothing.

One of the outside cats appeared, meowing and wrapping its way around his ankles, but he ignored it. He could pet the damn cat later. Right now, he had a girlfriend to find. He looked around. Her car was there, but her parents' house seemed to be dark, too. No one was home there either, at least that he could tell.

Where the hell were the McLains?

He and Iris had decided weeks ago to go to a Christmas ice skating show over in Franklin. He'd bought the stupidly expensive tickets that included a meal with the show.

He had everything he needed…except his Iris.

Angry now, he stomped back to his truck. After her cold shoulder and slamming the door in his face, it'd taken him a while to simmer down enough to go to sleep last night. He'd had every intention of pinning her down tonight and forcing her to answer his questions about what the hell was going on inside of that frustratingly beautiful head of hers, but now she had to pull a disappearing act on him.

If she didn't want to go to the damn ice skating show with him, she could've just said so. To stand him up like this was a class act of assholeness, in his opinion.

He threw his truck into reverse and spun out of the McLain's driveway. Fine. If she was going to be like this, he'd go do something else with his Saturday evening.

He chewed on his lower lip for a moment, and then it hit him – he could go buy propane for next year over at Frank's Feed. He'd been meaning to do that anyway. No time like the present.

Ignoring how pathetic it made him that he was going to spend his Saturday evening buying propane for next year's growing season rather than go on a hot date with a beautiful woman, Declan headed towards Frank's.

When he got there, he stormed inside and up to the counter. "I'd like to buy propane for next year," he growled at the pimply kid behind the counter.

"Yes, sir," the kid said. "Let me go grab the contract."

Declan ignored the pang of panic at the word "contract," and just nodded his head dismissively, as if he read contracts every day.

Thank God that wasn't actually true. He wasn't sure if he'd survive such tortures on a daily basis.

"Sorry to hear about your girlfriend," Mr. Burgemeister said at his elbow.

Declan jerked his head in surprise as he turned to stare at the older farmer. *Sorry to hear…? What is he talking about?*

"Tell her I hope she gets better soon," the old man continued.

Declan's mind raced. *Get better? Hold on, is this why her parents weren't home either?*

He debated demanding answers for a moment from the gentleman, but it was bad enough that he didn't know what was going on – he didn't need to inform Mr. Burgemeister of that fact also. And how the hell was it that Mr. Burgemeister knew and he didn't?!

"Thanks, I'll pass that along," he finally got out.

The kid reappeared from the back room, but Declan was already heading towards the front door. "Hey, you haven't signed the contract yet!" the kid hollered after him.

"I'll come back later!" he tossed back and then he headed outside, into the bitter cold.

He drove to the only place he could think of – Wyatt and Abby's house. She was a deputy sheriff for

Long Valley County. If anyone knew what was going on, it would be her.

He skittered to a stop on their gravel driveway after the longest drive of his life, and leaped out of his truck.

"It's a good thing I'm off duty so I don't have to arrest you for reckless driving," Abby observed wryly, standing on her front porch, cradling a mug of coffee in her hands.

Declan jerked his head in acknowledgment of her words, but started right into his burning question. "Do you know what happened to Iris?" he demanded.

"You don't know?" Abby asked, shocked. "I just figured someone would've told you."

"You don't know?" Wyatt repeated, coming out of the house and letting the screen door slam behind him with a bang. "I thought Stetson told you."

"Told me what?!" Declan practically hollered. If someone didn't talk to him and fast, he was going to start knocking heads together.

"Iris is at St. Luke's Hospital in Boise," Abby said quietly. "They life-flighted her out there this morning. I'm surprised you didn't hear the helicopter."

Declan staggered backwards, feeling like someone had punched him in the stomach. "Life flight?" he whispered.

"Oh God, I'm so sorry," Abby said, moving over to him and pulling him into a one-armed hug. "She fell while trying to clean off her front steps and hit her head on the concrete. Her mom was just coming out of her house when it happened, and thank God for that. It knocked Iris out cold and she could've ended up freezing to death."

Declan couldn't breathe. Couldn't think. Couldn't speak. Abby rubbed his back. "It's going to be okay," she said soothingly. "They've got her in the ICU—"

Intensive Care Unit. Life flight. Freezing to death.

Whatever else Abby said was lost to him as he sprinted towards his truck.

"Declan!" she called out but he was gone, tearing down their driveway like a madman.

He had to get to Boise. He had to find Iris. He had to make sure she was okay.

CHAPTER 31

IRIS

*O*H.

Her head.

Something was really wrong.

What was wrong? She didn't feel good.

At all.

Sweeping. She'd been sweeping. White stuff. Why was the dirt white? And outside? So cold.

She wasn't cold now, though. She was hot. She pushed the blankets away. "No, you have to keep them on you, Iris," her mom whispered.

"Mom?" she croaked out. She wanted to open up her eyes, but she didn't dare. It seemed like something bad would happen if she did. She just didn't know what.

White dirt? No, it'd been snow. She'd been outside, not in her kitchen. It came rushing back to her. She'd fallen on the front steps.

Everything ached. Everything hurt.

"I'm right here," her mom cooed, stroking Iris' hair away from her forehead. "Your dad and Ivy are, too."

She felt someone patting her. Was that her dad? She should open up her eyes. Her eyelids were just so heavy…

"You just hang in there, baby," her mom said. "I'm gonna step out and make a phone call and find out what Declan's number is, and I'll call and tell him to come visit you. That'll make you feel better. Ivy, darlin', come sit next to Iris while I—"

"No, Mom!" Iris got out. She struggled to get her eyelids open. She had to look at her mom. She had to get her mom to understand. "No Declan." But there were bright lights, and her eyes fluttered shut again, blocking out the pain.

No Declan. She'd fallen on her own front steps. If she'd been holding a baby…she could've killed it.

She couldn't be a mom. She couldn't be a wife. She couldn't love Declan.

It was better to just be done now, before she hurt anyone else.

CHAPTER 32

DECLAN

*H*E TORE TO A STOP in front of the St. Luke's Hospital ER. He slammed the door shut and sprinted towards the sliding doors.

"Sir, you can't leave your truck the—" The doors slid shut behind him, cutting off the words of the employee. Declan ignored them anyway. His entire life, he'd followed the rules; done what other people wanted him to do. He was the nice guy, through and through.

Where had that gotten him? A girlfriend who wouldn't talk to him, and was now in the ICU of the largest hospital in the state.

Screw the rules.

"Where is Iris McLain?" he barked at the plump, older woman sitting behind the reception desk. She looked up at him, calm as a cucumber.

"Spell the last name, please," she said, turning to her computer.

He barked it out as the employee from outside came jogging in. "Sir, you have to move your truck," he said, panting. He was quite heavy, and most definitely not used to running even short distances. Declan figured if it came to it, he could beat the guy in a foot race while hopping on one foot.

Ignoring the man as if he hadn't spoken, he turned back to the receptionist. "Room!" he practically hollered.

"She's still in the ICU, sir. Are you her husband?"

"No, but I oughta be," he snapped back. She just cocked an eyebrow at him. He growled in frustration. "She's been my girlfriend for years – since we were in high school together." He conveniently left out the part where he'd broken up with her because he was an idiot. "I was about to propose to her, and then she got hurt. Please, I have to see her."

"Your truck!" the heavyset man got in. Declan whirled on him and tossed his keys at the man's head.

"You want it moved – go move it yourself!" He turned back to the receptionist, ignoring the indignant sputterings of the man behind him that he was not a valet. "I have never loved a woman more than I love Iris Blue McLain," he told her. "Please, let me go see her."

She softened. "Down this hallway and to the left. Third door on the right."

Declan took off at a sprint, his cowboy boots pounding the tiles, echoing loudly. He brushed past doctors and a pair of nurses, intent only on finding

Iris. Apologizing for whatever it was that he'd done, and making the world better again.

It was all that mattered.

He skittered to a stop, almost falling on his ass on the slick tiles, and then stared at the door for a moment. Did he knock? He didn't know the proper protocol for an ICU hospital room. He raised his fist hesitantly, when the door opened. Ivy's face appeared right about where his knuckles were, and he drew back before he accidentally punched her in the face.

Wouldn't that be the cherry that'd top this sundae…

Instead of greeting him happily, her eyes went round and she looked horrified. She stepped out into the hallway and quickly pulled the door shut behind her. "What are you doing here?" she whisper-scolded.

"I came as soon as I heard. Not from anyone who should've told me, by the way." He glared at her for a moment. She had the decency to look ashamed.

"It wasn't my idea," she said softly. "I'm sorry, Dec, I really am. But Iris is refusing to see you. Mom was going to call you and tell you what had happened, and Iris told her no."

"No?!" Declan felt like he'd been punched in the stomach again. Twice in one day was just too much for one body to take, he reckoned, and he began to feel queasy. It'd be just his luck to start throwing up all over the hallway of the hospital.

"She didn't say why, but she was very, very clear

on the topic." Ivy let out a small, pained chuckle at that.

Declan just stared at her. Lost. Confused. *What the hell is going on?*

He wanted to take her by the shoulders and shake her until he got some answers from her, but as he looked down at her sweet face, so close in appearance to Iris' and yet not her at all, he realized that it wouldn't be fair. He needed to get some answers out of Iris; Ivy was just the middle man, and didn't appear to be any happier to be put in that position than he was to have her in it.

His shoulders dropped and he trudged back towards the front. "Declan!" Ivy called out. He spun around, his heart in his throat. Had Iris somehow changed her mind? Ivy simply looked at him for a moment and then said softly, "Don't give up on her yet. I know my sister can be exasperating, but she's always loved you. I think she always will. Don't give up on her yet," she repeated for emphasis.

He jerked his head once in acknowledgment and then continued his journey back up to the front. He had to find the security guard employee, apologize, retrieve his keys, and drive the winding, ice-covered road back home.

Without any more answers than he'd had before.

He was pretty sure he'd never felt so defeated in his life.

CHAPTER 33

DECLAN

He scooped the cat food out of the mouse-proof bin tucked up underneath the eaves of the house and dumped it into the weathered metal bowl. Two of the outdoor cats wound their way around his feet eagerly, while a third sat off to the side, regally inspecting the going-ons without actually getting involved. Declan had nicknamed him King last week, during his first trip over to feed the cats since the…

Since everything happened.

He refused to let himself think anything deeper than that.

He placed a bowl on the ground and the two eager cats dug into it, while King just continued to observe. He knew another bowl was coming.

Yup, he deserved that nickname all right.

"Come on, boy," he said, as he dug out the food

for the second bowl, "you know it wouldn't hurt you to say thanks every once in a while."

One long blink was his reply.

Declan wasn't sure how to interpret that, so instead, he simply put the bowl down on the ground. "Yours for the eatin'," he said gruffly.

Eleven days, and no word. He stared at Iris' front windows, the drawn curtains telling him nothing. Not that he expected them to. For all he knew, she was still in the ICU, clinging to life.

Surely she wasn't dead, though. Someone would've told him if she were dead.

Right?

Of course, he'd always thought that someone would've told him if she'd gotten into an awful accident and got life-flighted to Boise, and look at how that assumption had turned out.

He'd tried her front door the first few times he'd come over, and it'd always been locked. He could only hope that a neighbor had a key and was feeding Oreo and Milk. Surely someone would've thought to arrange for that…

After he'd come back from Boise, it'd taken him a while to calm down. Truth be told, he'd been pissed as hell at a certain Iris Blue McLain. First her yelling at him during the party, then crying, then slamming the door in his face, and then, the worst of all: Refusing to talk to him while she'd been in the ICU.

He'd calmed down, though that'd taken days to happen, and finally realized that whatever was going through her head, it made sense to her. He just needed a chance to figure out where the train had jumped the tracks, and rectify the situation. He'd probably screwed something up royally without realizing it – a talent he owned in spades – but he needed Iris to talk to him.

But until she came back home from the hospital, he could do nothing but feed her cats, and worry.

A position of helplessness that he detested.

A movement caught his eye, and he looked up to see the front door swing open to reveal Iris. Beautiful in a white sweater, she seemed to glow just a little. "Iris?" he whispered, taking a step forward. Was he imagining her? Was she his Christmas angel, come back to earth to tell him all the ways he'd screwed up their relationship?

Then he saw her cane, and thought that if she were an angel, she got the bum end of the deal. They were supposed to come back *perfect*, not still with shaky legs and an off-kilter way of looking at the world.

"I thought I heard something out here," Iris said softly. "It took me a while to get dressed and to the door. Sorry."

He moved closer, his breath forming clouds in the air in front of him, obscuring his vision a little, blurring her into an out-of-focus painting of a red-haired angel. But then the clouds dissipated, leaving him free to study her face closely.

To see the blue smudges under her eyes, and a flash of white in her hair. Quick as lightning, he moved over to her side to stare at the bald patch, covered over with a large white bandage.

"Oh, Iris," he said softly, his heart breaking as he stared at the bandage. Why hadn't he taken care of her? For the hundredth time, he wondered why he hadn't thought to come over and shovel her steps for her. He should've thought of it – a true gentleman would have.

"I'm getting tired," she said, just as softly. "Do you mind if we go inside and sit down?"

"Of course not!" he said, moving forward and looping his arm through hers.

As he shut the door behind them and helped guide her towards the couch, she said, "Thank you for thinking of feeding the outside cats. No one else would have, and then I would've broken my agreement with them." She grimaced slightly in what he assumed was supposed to be a smile. Milk and Oreo, disturbed from their afternoon nap, jumped off the couch and headed to the back bedroom. They appeared in perfect health, so someone had been taking care of them.

Good.

"Well, we couldn't have that," he said lightly, trying to make a joke out of her comment. He helped lower her to the couch and then stood back, unsure of what to do. Did she want him to leave? She looked worn out. He wanted answers – God, how he wanted answers – but he also couldn't pester her while she was so worn down. He could come back—

"Sit down," she said, patting the cushion next to her lightly.

Oh, thank God.

"Declan, I want to apologize," she said, cutting him off before he could marshal his thoughts together and really start grilling her for answers. Cut off at the pass, he snapped his mouth closed and simply stared at her.

He was finally going to get some answers.

Finally.

"I…You may or may not have noticed this," her mouth quirked for a moment, "but I am stubborn."

He bursted out laughing. He couldn't help himself. Describing Iris Blue McLain as being stubborn was rather like saying that a bull rider liked to take risks. Yes, that was true, but it didn't exactly sum the situation up in its entirety.

She glared at him for a moment, and then the corner of her mouth quirked up and her face broke out into a grin.

"Really, don't argue too heartily with that," she said with a sarcastic smile. "I'd hate for you to strain yourself, arguing so hard with me."

"Have you met you?" Declan finally got out around his laughter.

She stuck her tongue out at him. He grinned back.

"So anyway," she said with a huff of breath, "this whole thing," she waved her hand in the general direction of her cane, "has served to teach me that I have to learn how to swallow my pride. I just hate being dependent on other people. Hate it with a passion."

"Really? I hadn't noticed," Declan said dryly. She glared at him again. He grinned at her again, unrepentant. She rolled her eyes.

"I told my parents and Ivy that I didn't want to see you," she said quietly, and he sobered up to really listen to what she had to say. "I...didn't think that you'd want to be with someone who couldn't even sweep off their front doorstep without taking a helicopter ride afterwards."

He opened up his mouth to argue with her, and she just glared at him. He snapped his mouth shut again. If she wanted to talk, he had to let her talk. He could tell her how wrong she was when it was his turn.

"When I actually started to wake up and thus become a little more logical, my mom and Ivy talked me through it, and made me realize that I needed to tell you what I was thinking – what was going through my head – and then let you make the decision from there about what to do.

"So this is me being brave, and admitting that... Declan, I'm not perfect. I can't do everything. Your truck is going to be the death of me."

"What?!" he exclaimed, completely thrown off by the change in topic. "My truck?"

"Yes! It's big and tall and so damn hard to get up into. You help me, but every time, I almost land on my head on the dashboard. Well, I hate to be the one to tell you this, but I cannot date a farmer if I can't even get up into a pickup truck!"

He cut her off. "Now hold on a minute there, Iris. You just said that you're going to tell me the problems and then let me decide whether or not I care about them, and then you go and say things like that! You can't even last five minutes."

"Yes, but I can't get up into your truck. At least, not without making it into a death-defying stunt every time."

"Fine, but you're assuming that that matters to me. It doesn't. I can buy a little four-door car that's easy as pie to get into. Hell, I can take you car shopping with me and you can get in and out of every car on the lot, until you find one you like just right."

"You, drive a car? Farmers don't drive cars." She crossed her arms defiantly, as if stating an unbreakable law of the universe.

"I can't say I'll drive it out into the fields," he said dryly, "but I'm pretty sure they won't repo my farm if I happen to drive a car to pick up my girlfriend."

"Oh."

He let that soak in for a minute. For being as smart as she was, she sure did have some blindspots in her common sense.

"All right, fine. So you buy a car. But what about those ten kids you want?"

"Ten kids...oh, you heard what I was talking about with Stetson? Oh my God," he exclaimed, as everything clicked into place. "That's why you were so upset that night."

She gave a short nod, and he searched her face, trying to figure out what she was thinking. Did she want to marry him and have kids? He'd dumped her, rather abruptly, years ago. She hadn't brought it up since they'd gotten back together, but it was possible she was still harboring a grudge about it. He rather thought he would in her shoes.

Plus, getting married was a big step forward. Was she ready for that step? He knew what he wanted, but he'd known it pretty much all his adult life. He'd just been a bit dumber during certain parts of it, was all.

And anyway, she wouldn't want to marry him, not once she knew how stupid he was. What if dyslexia were passed on genetically? She wouldn't want stupid kids.

All in all, it was best to leave the discussion of marriage out of it. One step at a time.

"If you were just joking with your brother," she said, breaking into his thoughts, "and you don't want children with me, I understand." She'd obviously misunderstood his silence. Her back was so straight, she rather looked like she was going to snap off a salute to him at any moment.

"Sorry, sorry, trying to gather my thoughts." He reached out and took her hand, stroking her knuckles with his thumb. She relaxed.

Just slightly.

He decided to take that as a good sign, and

continued on. "I was joking with my brother about wanting ten kids, although if they're as cute as Flint, I might be talked into it."

He winked at her and she gave him a tentative smile in return. A thoroughly unconvincing smile.

"I don't mean to be a-pryin', but why does the idea of having kids upset you so much? In all the years I've known you, I've never seen you cry, and especially not in public. You promised to tell me what you were thinking and let me decide whether or not it was somethin' I could live with, right? Well, start talkin'. What's wrong with a couple of little ones running around?"

"I can't take care of kids!" she burst out defiantly, crossing her arms and glaring at him.

Well, if he'd wanted her to be forthright in her thoughts, he sure was getting it. "I have to admit that this kinda confuses me," he said slowly, reaching out and snagging one of her hands, pulling it towards him. "You're the most loving, sweet woman I've ever met. I figure you'll be the best mom this side of the Mississippi, and maybe the other, too. Why do you figure you can't have a baby?"

"Declan Miller, I've never met someone as smart *and* as stupid as you," she said, drumming the fingers of her free hand on the arm of the couch. Now that he had a hold of her other hand, he wasn't about to give it up for anything.

"Funny that – I had just about that same thought about you earlier in this conversation," he said dryly.

She glared at him for a moment, and then burst out, "What would've happened if I'd been holding Flint when I fell down on those steps out there? His head is still soft," she waved her free hand around the general vicinity of her head to indicate the problem area, "and instead of just knocking him out for a while, it would've killed him. I can't be trusted to hold a child."

He sat back and just stared at her for a long, long moment.

CHAPTER 34

IRIS

*D*ECLAN JUST STARED AT HER for the longest year of her life. Fine, maybe it wasn't actually a year, but it might as well have been. The agitation inside of her grew and grew. "Dec—" she exclaimed just as he said, "Well."

They both stopped.

"Let me go first," he said, before she could figure out where she was going with her outburst. She really hadn't gotten much past "Declan" in her mind anyway. She nodded regally, pretending as if she were bestowing a great gift upon him.

"You and your cat King," he muttered.

"What?" Her gaze shot over to the hallway that led down to her bedroom, where Milk and Oreo had disappeared.

"Nothing. Listen, I'll admit it – I hadn't thought about that. I should have. It's pretty obvious in retrospect. I'm still wrapping my head around your injuries and what they mean, long-term."

"Which is exactly my p—"

He cut her off with an exasperated, "Iris!"

She shut up.

She should probably let the man talk.

Even if it killed her in the process.

"Now, you've not wanted to talk a lot about your accident and injuries and I get that, but if we're gonna have a long-term discussion, I need to know certain things."

"Fair."

"First question first: Is your balance gonna be off for life? Or are you gonna get better? And how did your little helicopter ride affect things?"

She laughed a little at that one, and then sobered up quickly. "The original prognosis was that my balance would get better over time, as my brain re-learned to process information in a way that worked even with the damaged brain tissue in there. However, as you've already guessed, my little stunt outside didn't help matters. It was never a sure thing that I'd get my balance back completely, and it's even less certain now. As any brain surgeon will tell you, the brain is basically one big mystery, and the more they learn, the more they realize all that they still don't know. So it's pretty much one big crapshoot."

He nodded slowly, contemplatively. "Fair enough," he allowed. "So riddle me this, Iris McLain, is there any reason why we couldn't have a live-in nanny, who helped you take care of ten cryin' babies?"

She let out a short laugh and he grinned back, his straight white teeth gleaming, his eyes twinkling.

Damn, he was handsome. She could stare at that face for the rest of her life.

"Well," she said thoughtfully, doing her best to take his insane suggestion of a live-in nanny seriously, "first off, I think finding a live-in nanny who'd be willing to sign up for such an adventure would be plenty tough. Second, you seem to think that I can pop out ten babies all at once. Unless we're some sort of medical miracle in the worst sort of way, the chances are real high that the oldest baby would at least be ten years old by the time we're pushing out another newborn baby, preferably older than that if you wanted me to stay even slightly sane in the process."

"I will allow that my ten-baby comment was just me joking with my brother." *Oh thank God.* She could've cried with relief. "The question still stands, though – is there any reason you couldn't have at least one kid, if we also had a live-in nanny?"

She thought on that for a long moment. "Noooooo…" she finally said. "The doctors told me that I shouldn't have any problems conceiving or giving birth, as long as I didn't try to do something athletic on top of it, like run a triathlon. Truthfully, I think I should probably stay away from triathlons no matter what."

"There goes our plans for next week," Declan teased. She laughed. He grinned and squeezed her hand.

She quickly sobered up. "A live-in nanny could be real expensive, though," she worried, finally getting to the heart of the problem. Those were the kinds of luxuries that movie stars indulged in, not farmers' wives. "I have a lot of medical bills from the accident that I'm still paying off. How would—"

"There you go again, making assumptions," he teased. She shut up. "Truthfully, I've done real good for myself as a farmer. Potato and corn prices have been holding steady for a while, and I've stocked away cash. I had half-baked ideas about—well, that doesn't matter anymore. The bottomline is, I live pretty frugally. The mortgage is just about paid off on the house. I don't need much. If I had to pay for a live-in nanny, well, I'd just put less into the retirement fund, is all."

She was *quite* curious to hear more about his "half-baked ideas," but decided to leave that topic alone for the moment. She'd press him hard later on. Knowing Dec like she did, she refused to believe that he'd ever had a half-baked idea in his whole life.

Except maybe unleashing the plague of frogs down upon Mrs. Westingsmith's head. That stunt wasn't particularly well thought-out.

"I didn't realize you'd done so well for yourself," she said softly.

He shrugged, looking embarrassed. "It's not

somethin' you go around bragging about to every Tom, Dick, and Harry."

If she had to guess, she'd say he'd bragged to exactly *no one whatsoever*, but that wasn't shocking. Declan tended to take a body by surprise; it was easy to underestimate him because of how quiet and completely non-boastful he was.

Stupid hick farmer he was not.

She drew in a deep breath. It was time for her to confess her final failing. "Declan, I hate medical coding."

"You do?" he said, surprised. Or maybe he was just surprised by the topic change. It was hard to tell.

"Yes. With a passion. I've gone to the eye doctor twice now, and he's told me that either I give it up, or expect to go blind in the next year."

"Blind?!" he yelped. "Medical coding will make you *blind*?!"

Huh. On second thought, maybe that statement could use a bit more explanation.

"The accident. It threw off my balance, of course, and has made me weak as a baby when it comes to walking or standing for any significant amount of time, but my eyes…screens are the devil. It's gotten to the point where every screen is slightly doubled, even my cell phone. If I make myself look at a screen for too long, it eventually makes me nauseous and I have to stop so I can puke."

"Oh. My. God. Iris Blue McLain, how long has

this been going on?" Declan practically hollered at her.

Did holler at her.

She shrunk down in her seat. "A little while," she said in a soft voice.

He glared at her.

"A little lot while," she clarified.

He glared at her.

"Since the beginning," she mumbled.

He sank back into the couch, covering his eyes with his hands and mumbling something about "mule-headed women" but she decided to ignore that bit of commentary.

"I thought it'd get better," she said weakly.

"Is that what Dr. Mor told you when you went to him?" Declan asked pointedly.

Shit.

"Not exactly."

"So what exactly did he say? Other than you're working yourself into a state of blindness?"

Suddenly, the sleeve of her sweater was the most fascinating thing she'd ever laid eyes on. She began picking at the small loose fibers.

All right, she was avoiding looking at Declan.

He put his hand under her chin and lifted it up to look at him. She sighed.

"That this may or may not be a permanent state of being. That if I continue to push it, that I may go blind. That if I don't continue to push it, I may go blind. Basically, the same thing that the brain doctors all say – no one knows. The brain is a mysterious thing."

She snorted. If she heard that line one more time from a medical professional, she might be tempted to slug 'em. She'd been an RN for 13 years. They didn't need to tell her what she already knew – no one knew a damn thing.

Sure, there were more parts that they were less confused about than before, but that was about it. The brain was a giant black hole.

Which, for someone with a brain injury, was not a reassuring reality.

"Okay, Iris Blue McLain, then riddle me this one instead: What if you forgot about, just for a moment, your medical bills and money in general. What would you do instead?"

"Make canes," she blurted out, before her brain really even realized what she was saying. She clapped her hand over her mouth and sat staring at him, dumbfounded.

Make canes? Where did that *come from?*

But it was what she wanted. In the depths of her heart, when she was being completely unrealistic and bull-headed about the future, she'd lie in bed and dream. Since she'd started making her own canes, she was getting stopped in the store and on the street, people complimenting her on how beautiful and unusual they were. She loved having something unique and completely her.

Rather than having her cane define who she was

in a negative way, it'd become a badge of honor. A sign that she could still do something; was still worth something.

Canes were her independence and talents shining through to the world.

"Well now, Miss McLain, I swear you surprise me every day I am with you," Declan said with an easy grin. "Canes…it should've occurred to me, but sadly, I'll admit that it did not. Have you done research on selling them? When and where and for how much?"

"No. I never let myself get that far…it's just a silly daydream. I do have bills, and selling handmade canes isn't going to do it for me."

"I don't think that working yourself into a state of blindness is going to do it for you either," he said pointedly.

Dammit. He's right. I hate it when he's right…

"Have you talked to Dr. Mor about filing for disability?" Declan asked softly.

"I don't want to be on disability!" she shot back. And she didn't. She'd rather…well, do something real drastic that she'd think of later, than be on disability.

"Have you ever considered the fact that if you go on to disability now, it may be a temporary state of affairs, until your balance and your vision gets better, and you can work without making yourself sick? But if you continue to push yourself and you go blind, you will be on disability for life?"

Damn him to hell and back. She hated it when

people thought of blindingly obvious things that she'd never considered.

No pun intended.

"No," she whispered, dropping her eyes to her lap, fiddling her thumbs together, avoiding his gaze.

"Iris, darlin', it isn't a crime to need help every once in a while, truly it isn't. You've spent your whole life helping other people. Helping me with Spanish. Helping defend your sister against those two hooligans in high school. Helping patients at the hospital in Pocatello. You've done nothing but help other people from the word 'go.' You have to start letting other people help you. It's not a character defect to need help in return for all you've done for this world."

She nodded, shutting her eyes tightly. She needed a moment to make herself accept what he'd said as a fundamental truth, even if it went against every bone in her body.

He pulled her to him, and stroked her back softly. "I'm so happy you're home," he whispered, and then he was scooping her up into his arms and she was snuggling against his broad chest as he carried her to her bedroom and laid her down on the bed, pulling her against him and drifting off to sleep together.

∼

His hands were following the curve of her hip as he woke up, need pushing him to explore her body, even in his sleep.

He gently rolled her over onto her back, and began nibbling his way up her side, whispering to her as he went. The shadows in the room kept it private and safe, a place he could do and say what he wanted without any fear.

She murmured, moving her legs restlessly against the sheets, and he wondered if she was awake, or in a dream state. He hoped that if she were dreaming, they were very good dreams.

"I love you," he whispered into the stillness, running his tongue over her adorable outie belly button. "I love you so much, Iris."

"I love you, too," she whispered back.

His heart stopped. She was awake. And she'd heard him. And she loved him, too.

What a glorious feeling that was.

He pulled himself up so he was hovering over her lips. "You heard me," he whispered. "I thought you were still asleep."

"Would you have said those words if you thought I was awake?" she whispered back, laughter in her voice.

"Probably."

Not. He was a wimp when it came to that kind of thing. He'd put in an 18-hour day on a tractor without blinking an eyelash, but telling a woman he loved her?

Even a woman as amazing as Iris? Even as many times as he'd said it before – years before?

Yeah, it was scary.

But she'd said she loved him back, which had to be some sort of miracle. Now all he had to do was never, ever let her know just how broken he was.

She may love him, but only because she thought he was whole. A real man didn't have unforgivable flaws.

A real man wasn't dyslexic.

He kissed her again, running his tongue over her lips before she let him in with a sigh of happiness. "I guess it's time I showed you just how much I love you," he whispered, once he pulled back.

And then he did.

CHAPTER 35

DECLAN

*D*ECLAN WAS ROUGH CHOPPING some potatoes and carrots for dinner when the landline rang. Picking the phone up from the cradle, he tucked it under his cheek.

"Hello?" he said, moving back to the cutting board.

"Dec, you would not believe what just popped up on Facebook!" Iris squealed in his ear.

He grinned into the phone. Whatever was making Iris this happy was A+ in his book. "They finally found Bigfoot," he guessed, tongue in cheek.

She paused for a moment, decided he was kidding, and plowed on as if he hadn't said anything. "Piglets! Mr. Harther got an early crop of them, and his granddaughter took pictures and put them up on Facebook. Oh Declan, you should see them. They are adorable! I already called and asked how much they are, and they're not expensive at all. He said that for you, he'd—"

"No!"

The sound came out harsh and rough and rude but he hadn't been able to stop himself.

There was silence, dead silence, on the line.

Declan laid down the knife next to the chopping board and rubbed his eyes wearily with the palms of his hands. "Millers are farmers, not pig farmers, Cookie. There's a difference. I—"

"Don't Cookie me, Declan!" she snapped, cutting him off at the pass. "Someday, you're going to tell me why the hell you refuse to get into the one thing you've always loved and adored. Don't patronize me in the meanwhile."

And then she hung up.

Dammit.

Dammit, dammit, dammit.

Declan dropped the phone to the counter and stared sightlessly at his cutting board and his half-finished dinner.

It'd been about three months since he'd finally knocked some sense into Iris, and convinced her to apply for disability. She actually had, which Declan had been shocked to see happen. He would've bet good money on the fact that she wouldn't go through with it, but she had. With those checks coming in and living in her parents' MIL apartment, she was barely squeaking by.

He'd offered to pay for her medical bills, to take

those payments off her plate, but Iris hadn't changed that much. She was bound and determined to pay the bills off all on her own.

She'd been making canes, perfecting the art and craft of it, and researching where and how to sell them, and had moved on with her life.

He hadn't moved on with his, though.

He knew it. He knew he'd done nothing but ignore the reality haunting him: He couldn't propose to Iris until he told her the truth about him. It wasn't fair to her to shackle herself to him for the rest of her life, if she didn't know just how stupid he was.

And, how stupid he could make their kids. He still didn't know if dyslexia was a genetic thing, and without revealing that he had it, he couldn't think of a good reason to ask someone to do the research for him and tell him the answer.

So he'd just been drifting along, happy to take Iris out on dates, make love to her, and then leave her at her house as he drove back to his.

Two weeks ago, Wyatt had told him point-blank that it was "time to shit or get off the pot," and then mumbled something about telling Abby thanks for that bit of advice. Declan had stared at him for a moment, but had decided to let it pass.

And anyway, he and Iris were both 35, and if they were gonna have even a small fraction of his 10-kid posse he'd joked about, they probably should get a move-on.

Which meant marriage.

And telling her the truth.

Which led him right back to his current predicament.

He'd been much happier ignoring all of this, of course. If she knew and chose to break up with him because of it...

He wasn't quite sure he'd live through the heartache.

But if she gave up on him and moved on without him because he refused to move their dating relationship up to marriage level, well...

He wasn't quite sure he'd live through the heartache of that, either.

With a growl, he pulled out his cell phone and dialed Austin's number. "Hey," he said as soon as Austin picked up, "you got time to come on over here and chat for a minute?"

~

Austin was quick to show up, something Declan was grateful for. He was pacing around in his barn like a caged animal when he heard tires on the gravel driveway. He headed outside to meet Austin at his truck. The weak spring sunshine felt good on his shoulders. It was a relatively peaceful spring day – no rain and only a light breeze – which was some kind of record for Long Valley. He would enjoy it while he could take it.

They shook hands and then Austin looked

around. "You need help fixin' your combine for next season?" he asked.

"Oh no, I gave up on that piece of shit. I've already signed the paperwork with the bank for a new one for next season." He dug his toe into the rain-softened gravel and then said with a fake cheerfulness, "What about a ride?"

"Sure," Austin said, his brow creasing with confusion. Being the kind of guy he was, though, he didn't demand answers, but rather just followed along behind Declan into the barn, where they saddled up his two horses, Hero and Badlands, in companionable silence.

This was good for the horses anyway. Just coming out of winter, they'd been cooped up for far too long. They'd enjoy a good ride.

Anything to justify putting this off for just a little longer.

Declan decided to ignore that thought, too.

They rode out along the fields, his hard wheat just starting to peek out of the ground. The brilliant green of the softly rolling hills sang spring to his soul, and he took a deep breath, inhaling the sunlight and faint warmth and pure Idahoness of the air.

They stopped at a stream, letting their horses drink as they listened to a few bullfrogs singing, when Declan finally blurted out, "I'm dyslexic."

Austin sat still for a good long while, not saying anything, not moving, and Declan just let him process it. He didn't get antsy with him like he would have with anyone else; this was just the way that

Austin internalized information before actually responding.

"Well now, that makes a lot of sense," Austin finally said, tipping his hat back on his head and looking over at Declan.

"It does?" Declan said, surprised. Out of all of the things that he thought Austin would say...well, that particular response wasn't even in the top 10.

"I'd never met a person more averse to reading and studying than you," Austin said with a small grin. "I thought you just weren't fond of school. I wasn't either, but...you could avoid studying better than even me, and I thought I had it down to a science."

Declan remembered all of the Friday nights...and Saturday nights...and okay, Monday, Thursday, and Sunday nights...all right, Tuesday and Wednesday nights too...where he'd done his best to convince Austin that they ought to go out on the town or go for a hike or hell, go to the grocery store – anything instead of studying.

In retrospect, he probably wasn't the world's best roommate.

"So why now?" Austin asked simply.

Declan knew what he was asking – *why are you telling me this now?*

Which was a perfectly valid question to ask.

"Iris," Declan replied. "I want to ask her to marry me, but I have to tell her how stupid her future husband really is, before she agrees to take me on."

"And...?" Austin prompted.

"And what?"

"Well, why are you telling me this? Shouldn't you be asking Iris? It's up to her, not me," he said with a chuckle.

"Yeah. I know. I just...I don't know how to tell her."

Which as soon as he said it, he felt ridiculous. He knew what Austin was going to say, and he didn't disappoint. "I'd suggest starting with the fact that you're dyslexic," Austin said dryly, "and go from there."

When Declan started to mumble about how helpful Austin was being, Austin cut him off with a wave of the hand. "Declan, how long have you known Iris?"

"About all my life." He honestly couldn't remember meeting her. She was just there, always. He hadn't noticed her as a girl until junior high, but they'd been in most of the same classes in elementary school, and anyway, Sawyer was small enough that even if they weren't in the same classroom, they saw each other in passing on the playground, field trips, and other school activities. She was usually busy thumping the other boys into submission in any sport they dared to challenge her to.

"How long have you loved her?"

"Since junior high." The first junior high dance. Eighth grade. He'd spotted her across the gym, chatting with some of her friends, and he felt like he'd been gut punched. He'd never seen such a beautiful girl in all his life, with her hair curled and piled up on top of her head. She looked so grown-up, and so at ease, so confident.

He instantly became tongue-tied, a condition that persisted around her until their tenth grade year together.

"And in all the time you've known her, how often have you seen Iris be downright mean to someone?"

"Once." Declan grinned at the memory. "Oh, but they deserved it. Ezzy and Tiffany had ganged up on Ivy, and Iris let 'em have it. She told them what she thought of them, their parentage, and exactly what items they could shove where the sun don't shine."

Austin chuckled at that. "I think I would've paid good money to see that," he said.

Declan nodded. "Truly one of Iris' shining moments. I didn't know she even knew some of those words." He sobered up. "But what if—"

"Declan, you need to pull your head out of your ass," Austin said, not even letting Declan finish stating his worry. "I wasn't there when y'all were going to school, so I didn't get to see your courtship and whatnot. But I have seen you since she moved back to Long Valley, and Dec, I've never seen you so happy in my life. She loves you, truly loves you.

"Don't be a dumbass and screw that up."

Declan nodded and swallowed hard. Austin was right. Of course.

It was just easier said than done.

CHAPTER 36

IRIS

*I*RIS PACED around her living room, stopping every few feet to growl in the general direction of her phone. It'd been hours since she'd hung up on Declan, and instead of calming down, she found she was just getting more riled up.

Without warning, her mind flashed back to their first date since she returned to Long Valley, where she'd wanted to pace around while waiting for him to show up, but hadn't dared. She smiled to herself, happy at least that she'd progressed to the point that she dared to pace her living room without a cane, without worrying about taking a tumble. Her balance was coming along quite splendidly, according to the doctor, and even according to her own high internal standards.

Someday, she might be back to normal. Maybe.

But what was not coming along was her relationship with Declan. Stetson had proposed to

Jennifer after knowing her for two weeks, and Wyatt had made a move on Abby damn quickly, too.

Whereas Declan had had years now – their entire lives, actually – and still wasn't ready to make a move.

It was enough to make a girl want to wring some necks. Specifically, necks in the possession of Declan Miller.

A knock at her front door pulled her out of her thoughts, and her heart instantly jumped into her throat. It could be Declan, finally ready to tell her what the hell was going on in that head of his, or it could be one of her parents wanting to chat, or just a friend stopping by.

Please, God, let it be...

She pulled the door open.

Declan stood there.

Oh, thank God.

But in his hands, he was holding up...

"*Pigs for Dummies?*" Completely confused, she read the title out loud, and then moved her eyes up to Declan's, his dark brown eyes studying her face carefully. When he didn't say anything, she held the door wide open and gestured to him with a sweep of her hand. "C'mon in," she said, the sweet spring air following him into the house. She started to close the door but decided on second thought to leave it open.

It was lovely outside, and she needed some of that loveliness right now.

"Cookie, I'm sorry," Declan said softly, laying the *Dummies* book down on her rocking chair and turning to take her hands into his. He brought them up to his mouth and placed a kiss on her knuckles. "You're right. About everything."

He blew out a breath and said quietly, "I need to tell you something, and you may hate me for keeping this from you all this time, but you have to know before you make any choices about your future."

She nodded slowly, keeping her eyes pinned on him. Whatever it was, it was huge. Declan's face didn't look like this because he wanted to confess he'd turned in a library book three weeks late. She wasn't going to like it, that much was clear.

Had he had a fling while he was up at the U of I, and had a secret love child stashed away up there? Was he cursed with some dread disease and was going to die in six months? Did he dream about starting a rock band and wanted to run away to LA?

Please don't let it be LA. She couldn't handle living in Los Angeles…

Turns out, she could imagine a lot of awful scenarios if left to her own devices, and she quickly began to wish that he'd hurry up and tell her what had him tied up in such knots, so she could only worry about one awful scenario instead of all of them.

"I am dyslexic."

The words were a bombshell in the quiet of the house, but even as part of Iris' mind spun with shock, the other part was tallying things up – tiny, isolated events that hadn't made sense until just then.

Him begging her to read his Spanish vocabulary out loud instead of making him do it. Refusing to put together flashcards, saying that they never helped him much. Studying the menu at a new restaurant carefully, and then ordering the same dish as her. Asking her what her class schedule was going to be, and then "coincidentally" having virtually the same class load as her.

Like the spinning of a lock on a safe, the last item clicked into place, and Iris looked back up at him. "You are so damn smart," she breathed, staring at him with admiration.

"What?!" he stuttered. She could tell he'd been bracing himself for a reaction – any reaction – except for that one.

"Your coping skills are out of this world, you know that? Dammit, Declan, I cannot believe that as your tutor for four years, I never knew. Oh!" she yelped as the memory washed over her. "Lordy, no wonder you didn't want to help me study my medical codes!" she exclaimed, laughing and clapping her hand over her mouth as she re-imagined that scenario from his point of view. "You ran out of here like your ass was on fire, and I was so damn confused. Meanwhile, you were so worried…you thought I'd think you were stupid, didn't you?"

"Iris, I am stupid," he said in that explaining-the-facts-of-life-to-a-small-child voice that she hated. She rather thought he was going to reach his hand out and pat her condescendingly on the head.

She beat him to it, and whacked him upside the head instead. "Oww!" he howled, rubbing the spot and staring at her in shock. "What was that for?"

"For being an idiot," she informed him. "Declan, you're not stupid. You're an idiot, but you're not stupid."

He tilted his head to the side and said dryly, "Well gosh, now I feel better."

She ignored him.

"Dyslexia is mostly found to be a genetic disease," she told him. "So—"

"I was afraid of that," he breathed, cutting her off, his eyes wide. "Oh God, Iris, I can't have kids. I can't make them stupid like me."

She hit him upside the head again.

"Declan!" she hollered. "You're going to listen to me if I have to hogtie you to a chair with a gag in your mouth to make it happen."

"*Hog*tie?" he repeated, a grin breaking out across his face, despite the seriousness of the situation. "At a time like this, you're making jokes? I know you want me to raise pigs, but I think this is a little extreme."

She ignored his attempts at levity. She was not going to let him sidetrack her. "Were you ever officially diagnosed with dyslexia?"

He shook his head slowly, his smile fading from his face. "You're only the second person – no, third person I've ever told about this," he admitted.

She wondered for a moment who the other people

were, and then decided to leave it alone for the moment. They had bigger fish to fry.

"There's a lot they can do for people with dyslexia," she said softly, reaching out and stroking his cheek. "The younger they realize that there's a problem, the more they can do. Unfortunately, because boys tend to struggle with sitting still in class and school in general, learning disabilities are sometimes mistaken as simply 'boys being boys' and are not treated, when in fact, the boys are struggling with understanding the work being put in front of them. No one likes being bored."

He nodded. "Elementary school was okay, because there was recess and art class and PE, but by the time we got into junior high…I hated school. I got through it by being the nicest kid in class. The teachers all loved me – except Mrs. Westingsmith, of course. She never forgave me for those frogs – and so I think some of them passed me out of pure pity. They didn't want to be the cause of a 'nice boy like me' being held back."

"Yet another example of your coping skills, Dec. You made up for not being able to read by becoming the best-behaved boy in class. The teachers loved you. That meant they were more likely to give you special attention, even in a classroom full of students who needed help, and even if they couldn't drill reading into your head, they still passed you because they liked you.

"Which isn't a ringing endorsement of our

educational system, that's for sure, but Declan, it is a ringing endorsement of your coping skills."

She took his hand and walked him over to the couch and sat him down, staring at him intently. She felt like if she could just drill her eyes straight into his, he could truly understand what she was about to tell him, and take it to heart.

"They've done studies of twins, and even with one twin having dyslexia, the chances of the other twin having it too are only about 60% or so. Dyslexia is right in there with brain injuries – the scientists know more about what they don't know, than what they do know. The more they learn, the more they realize what they still have left to learn.

"The important part that you need to worry about, Declan, is that it isn't a life sentence. It isn't any indication of your intelligence level. It's simply your brain pathways not connecting correctly. You didn't screw up. You're not stupid. And you don't have to hide it. It simply is what it is."

"I've always hated that saying," he said in a tremulous whisper.

"Me too," she admitted with a grin. "With a passion. Knowing that something was out of my control? Worst feeling ever." She sobered up and asked quietly, "So your whole song and dance about Millers being row crop farmers, not pig farmers…you were intimidated by the idea of learning something new?"

He nodded, his chocolate brown eyes growing

even darker. "My dad taught me how to grow crops. I've been trained for this career my whole life. And if a new question pops up, I ask Austin or a seed salesman or my brothers. I don't have to learn anything new, not from the ground up, that is. It's... terrifying to think about learning about something so completely different."

"But you want to." She said it as a statement, not a question, but he nodded anyway.

"Pigs are so damn smart. Way smarter than I'll—"

She whacked him upside the head.

"They're really smart animals, just like me," he finished dryly.

She grinned at him. "You're getting better by the minute. Any day now, you'll actually realize that you're one of the smartest men I know." He shot her a doubtful look and she winked. "After all, you had the smarts to fall in love with me."

He laughed and his arms shot out to pull her close against him. She tumbled against his plaid button-up shirt-covered chest, breathing in the scent that was masculine and amazing and all Declan.

"I'd love to help you learn about pigs," she said, muffled against his strong chest. "I could sit and read *Pigs for Dummies* out loud to you while you cooked dinner. This seems like a fair division of labor to me!" She could feel his laughter vibrate through his chest.

"I should've known that getting out of cooking was going to end up in this conversation somehow," he groused jokingly. He held her tight against him, stroking his hands through her hair lightly.

"It was so tough, growing up dyslexic," he said softly into the quiet room. "I don't know if I could bear to put a child through that."

"Well," she said, pulling back a little and looking him straight in the eye, "first off, we'll know to look for the signs, instead of just letting the kid flounder. Second, although your kids will be genetically more likely to be dyslexic than if they're born to parents without dyslexia, it really isn't a for-sure thing. All of us have positives and negatives that we're going to pass on to our kids. I mean, just think – some poor kid is going to be 'blessed' with my sense of direction! They're gonna get lost at every recess."

He laughed quietly at that, and she grinned back at him. Her heart swelled so big, she wasn't sure it'd stay contained in her chest. "Declan Miller, I love you. All of you. Your thoughtfulness, your work ethic, your moral code, your huge heart. And your brains. I don't know that I've ever met someone as good as you at dealing with the shitty hand life gave you, and still continuing on with a smile on your face."

He let out a roar of laughter and she jerked back in surprise. "What?" she asked, cocking her head to the side in confusion.

"You…" he gasped. Finally, he sat up straight and reached out to cup her face in his hands. "Iris, I could say exactly the same thing about you – word for word." She opened up her mouth to argue – after all, her injuries only happened in the last year; she hadn't been cursed with them her whole life like he had – but he placed a finger against her lips to stop her. "I know you don't see you the way I do, or hell, the way the rest of the world does. But please believe me when I say that you are truly something special, Iris Blue McLain."

He fumbled around in his pocket for a moment, until he finally found something and pulled it out.

A small, felt-covered box.

Oh God, oh God, oh God...

He scooted off the couch and onto the floor, dropping to one knee and looking up at her. "I bought this ring a long time ago." *Breathe, Iris, just breathe...* "Back when we were at college together, actually. I know it seems like if I'd had this ring for that long, I could come up with a more elaborate proposal than this, but Iris, I've finally realized that none of that matters. All that matters in this world is that you love me. Iris, will you marry me?"

She threw herself forward, wrapping her arms around his neck and kissing him again and again, crying tears of joy as she whispered, "Yes, yes, yes," between every kiss.

Finally, she was home, where she wanted to be.

She was in Declan's arms. And that was all that mattered.

CHAPTER 37

DECLAN

*D*ECLAN SHIFTED from one foot to the other impatiently, waiting for Iris to show up. She'd been damn mysterious in her text messages, asking him to meet her at The Glade at one o'clock, and his curiosity was growing stronger by the minute.

He'd known what she'd meant by The Glade, of course. In high school, when they'd been caught one too many times by parental figures in some...pretty heavy duty make-out sessions, they'd started trying to find new places to neck.

Ones where parents were less likely to stumble in on them.

It had been a search for just such a place when Iris had caught her foot on a tree branch and had fallen down a ravine, breaking her leg.

Whoops.

As soon as her leg healed, they were right back at it. They'd finally found this place – a beautiful clearing in amongst the pine trees with a small creek bubbling past – and had christened it on the spot. It was where they'd lost their virginity to each other, actually.

Yeah, he wasn't likely to forget about The Glade any time soon.

It was three weeks until the wedding, and Declan was also deep into planting and taking care of his new piglets. In other words, they had about three seconds to spare per day for each other, before falling, exhausted, into bed each night. Maybe Iris was feeling neglected, and wanted some alone time with him.

He shifted on his feet again. He was happy to give her what she needed, but she also needed to show up. If he didn't see a head of gorgeous red and golden hair making its way towards him in the next five minutes, he'd be forced to go back to work and try this again later.

But just before he gave up and started the long trek to his truck, he saw the glow of her hair and grinned to himself. She'd made it. He headed towards her, jogging through the underbrush to make it to her side quickly. She stopped and grinned at him when he finally made it. "Are you that…quiet while hunting?" she asked dryly. "If so, may I suggest some changes to your hunting strategies?"

He laughed.

"Some prey have already been caught," he informed her pertly, and then leaned down to give her a quick peck on the lips.

Well, what he intended to make a quick peck on the lips. Minutes later, he finally made himself pull away. Her eyelashes fluttered open and she looked at him with a dreamy smile on her face. "Hi," she breathed.

"Hey," he whispered back. He took the blanket and small basket from her arms, leaving her with just her handmade walking stick, and together, they wandered towards The Glade. A part of him wanted to push her for information – to have her tell him right away what was going on; why she insisted on doing this now – but even he realized that letting her sit down and get comfortable before he started peppering her for info would be a good idea.

No matter how curious he was.

He laid out the blanket on a patch of soft green grass, just poking up into the spring air, and helped her settle in before opening the basket up to peer inside. He found containers from Betty's Diner and a couple of small ones from The Muffin Man.

"I see you've been cooking again," he teased her.

She threw her head back and laughed. "I make a shitastic farmer's wife-to-be, don't I?" she said dryly. "I think I'm going to have to skip the pie baking contest for the county fair this year."

And every year.

But he decided to keep that particular thought to himself. Finding someone who could cook was easy. Finding someone who made him as happy as Iris did? Impossible.

He should know. He tried to do just that for 15 years, and failed miserably.

They settled in, dishing out the food and then mumbling to each other about how good it was around bites of it. Finally, they'd cleaned out the two dessert containers – which had contained chocolate cheesecake for her and apple pie for him – and there was nothing left to do but tackle the elephant in the room.

Or glade, as the case may be.

"So," he said quietly, and he could feel the air change around them when he said it – the easy, relaxed atmosphere instantly morphing into stiffness and worry. He plowed ahead anyway. This had to be big enough to make it worth it to push through. She wouldn't have pulled him away from farming; she wouldn't have pulled herself away from her business and from planning their wedding, if it wasn't truly dire. "I'm guessing you wanted to chat with me about something?"

She sent him a weak smile. "Am I that transparent?" she asked quietly.

"As Saran Wrap," he confirmed.

She grimaced.

He laughed.

"I've…been telling myself to talk about this for a long time," she started out quietly. His chest tightened in panic. Maybe she'd changed her mind about dyslexia. Maybe she'd done more research and had decided that dyslexia really does make a person stupid and she really shouldn't marry him, and—

"We need to talk about why we broke up all those years ago."

His panic instantly changed directions. This wasn't the topic he'd been panicking about, but it might as well have been. He didn't want to talk about this either, because…

Well, because it was an awful time in his life. He didn't exactly want to think about it very hard. Why was it that girls wanted to talk about things so much? Couldn't they just forget about stuff and move on? He—

She put her hand out on his arm, jerking him out of his thoughts. "I know this isn't an easy topic to discuss. There's a reason why I've held off talking about it until now. I am a giant chicken, and I wanted to just forget and move on. But Declan, we lost 15 years of our lives that we could've spent together but didn't, because of whatever it was that caused you to break up with me, and I can't help but worry that whatever it was will rear its ugly head again."

She drew in a deep breath. "What if I accidentally step in it – just splash around in the deep end and cause all sorts of problems, without even knowing that I'm doing it? I can't risk it. I can't risk our marriage by ignoring this between us. If I don't find out what caused you to break up with me before, then I can't keep it from causing you to divorce me in the future."

That wasn't possible, of course. What had

happened before…well, it was literally impossible to be a repeat event.

But the bigger issue…

Well, he knew she was right, dammit all. As much as he hated to admit it, she was. Why did she have to make sense all the time?

He closed his eyes and groaned.

"Is it really that bad?" she asked quietly. Her hand was stroking its way up his arm and he reached over with his other hand to take it into his.

"Yes."

It was silent then, with only the distant bubbling of the brook and an industrious frog croaking out its thoughts. He opened his eyes and stared at her for a moment.

He had no choice. He had to tell her.

Even if she hated him for it.

"I killed my mom," he said into the stillness.

CHAPTER 38

IRIS

$\mathcal{S}$HE STARED AT DECLAN, her eyes round, her mouth a perfect O. She didn't know what to say to that. She wasn't quite sure there was anything to say to that.

He couldn't mean that he took a gun and shot her, obviously. Declan would never do that. Her mind scrambled to remember the details. His mom had died in a car wreck outside of Boise. Declan had been at home with Iris in Pocatello when he'd gotten the call. He couldn't have killed his mom. He wasn't within 200 miles of her when she died.

"I don't understand," she finally whispered, when it became clear he wasn't going to say anything else.

He rubbed his eyes with the palms of his hands, looking twenty years older. Haggard.

"I told her about being dyslexic," he said, so quietly, she almost couldn't hear him above the water and the frog and the light rustling of the leaves in the wind. "I was struggling. Do you remember that? Even with your help, I was just pulling in a D in a couple of my classes."

She nodded. She did remember that now. She'd forgotten – lost in the mists of time. He'd made jokes at the time about how Ds get degrees. She'd known he was trying to cover up his frustration about not doing well – that he was using humor to play it down – but she hadn't realized just how much it was really bothering him.

He truly was gifted at hiding his worries, if that could be considered a gift.

She wanted to tell him that he should've told her what was going on, that she would've wanted to know so she could help even more.

But now was not the time for that. He needed to get this off his chest. It was his time to talk, and her time to listen.

"I called my mom, and I whined," he said with a small smile. "I was 20, and maybe some people would consider me to be an adult, but I wasn't. Not really. You know that Mom and I were always close. Closer than Dad and I ever would be. Dad had Wyatt, and then years later, Stetson. He taught me how to farm, but Mom...she taught me how to *be*. How to be an adult. How to be a gentleman. How to love.

"And when I called to vent my frustrations, it just sorta slipped out. I hadn't meant to tell her, but I did, and...she went into mom mode. She told me that I was smart and kind and all of those things moms are supposed to tell their kids, and then she decided to surprise me. She made a batch of pumpkin chocolate chip cookies – my favorite, of course – and packed them into the car and took off. I'm not even sure if she gave Dad a chance to say yes or no to the idea. She was going to come over to see me – drive across the state to bring me cookies – and…just be there for me."

He stopped. He grew so quiet for so long, Iris wasn't sure he was going to start talking again, but finally, he continued.

"I didn't know what she was doing until I got that phone call from Dad. He was frantic. The police had just called to let him know that she was being life-flighted to Boise, and he wanted me to come help him take care of things. You were there. You know how that conversation went."

She nodded slowly. How quiet Declan had been that day after she got home from her classes. How he'd answered the phone with a smile, and then how that smile had faded away into a frown and then full-blown panic as the conversation continued.

She'd been so confused, watching him. What was happening? She couldn't hear his dad's voice clearly enough to know what he was saying, but she could tell that whatever was going on, his dad was upset. It wasn't a very long conversation, but…

It had changed everything. She didn't want to make his mother dying all about her, of course, but that day cost her Declan. She didn't know it at the time, but he'd never be the same around her again. It wasn't too much longer after his mom's funeral that he broke things off with her.

"Declan, you told your mom that you were dyslexic. You didn't kill her. There's a—"

"Don't you think I've told myself that? I know the truth. Logically. Up here." He tapped the side of his head, the pain etched across his features. "But..."

He just sat there, the weight of it all physically crushing him down.

"Why didn't you tell me?" she whispered.

"And kill you, too?" He let out a short laugh. "I'd just killed my mother by admitting my weakness to her, and you think I should've fixed that by admitting my weakness to you, too?"

He stood up and strode around the glade, stomping through the bright green grass, shoving his hands into his hair. "I didn't even tell my brothers what happened. My dad never did ask why Mom was so hell-bent on making it over to see me that day. His whole world had just been destroyed by the hoof of a deer. He didn't have the mental capacity to ask me questions, and for that, I was glad. I don't know what I would've told him if he'd asked."

The hoof of a deer...

Iris had forgotten that detail. The deer had hit the grill of the car and twisted, sending the right front hoof straight through the windshield and into Declan's mother's forehead. The chances of that happening...if the deer had just twisted a little further to the side...

The whole thing was an awful story, too awful to be real.

Except it was.

No wonder Declan had thought it was the gods, exacting their revenge on him for admitting his weaknesses.

She stood up and moved to his side, throwing her arms around him. "Oh Dec. I wish I'd known..."

So much made sense now. His complete refusal to tell her why he was breaking up with her. Moving up to northern Idaho, far away from friends and family. He'd stopped responding to her phone calls, and eventually, she'd just given up. Whatever had caused him to do what he did, she couldn't fix it if he wouldn't even talk to her.

"Declan, you have to know here," she touched his heart, "that you didn't do anything wrong. You *have* to believe it. You were just as innocent as everyone else."

"But then you hit a deer too, and this happened," he said, gesturing at her legs. "Maybe God is trying to tell me something. Maybe I shouldn't be trusted to be in people's lives. Maybe I should just be single and protect those I love from...me."

She pulled away and frowned at him.

"Declan Miller, you sure can be a dumbass sometimes," she said bluntly. He stared at her, his mouth agape. "According to you, all you have to do is break up with me and stay single for the rest of your life, and that will somehow protect me from getting hurt? Need I remind you that this happened," she gestured towards her legs, "while we were broken up? So I'm not sure how breaking up again will protect me from the terrible things that happen in life."

She dropped her hands down by her sides and planted them on her hips. "If you think that I'm going to allow you to hide from your fears again, well, you've got another think a-comin'! I won't put up with it, Declan, not for one minute. You pushed me out of your life before, and I'm not going to allow it again." She crossed her arms over her chest and glared at him. "Now quit being a dumbass."

"But…" he said weakly.

She leaned up on her tiptoes and kissed him. "Did you ever go see someone after your mom's death?" she asked quietly as she pulled away. He shook his head slowly. "Let me guess: You didn't think a 'real man' should go talk to a counselor?" He nodded, even more slowly. She rolled her eyes. "You are such a guy sometimes," she informed him, and a puff of laughter escaped his lips. "Seriously though, you'd never catch a girl thinking that counseling is unnecessary and that they just have to tough through the awful things in life."

He cocked an eyebrow at her and said dryly, "No, but I bet you I could find a girl who thinks that she ought to work herself into a state of blindness in order to pay down her medical bills."

"Touché," she grumbled, and he grinned. "Fine,

so we *both* have things we need to work on. The point is, I've worked on my shit. It's time for you to work on yours."

He pulled her against him, tucking her head against his chest as he held her in his arms. "Yeah, you're right," he said softly. "Everyone thinks of Wyatt as being the one in the family who needs help. People think that I have the easy life. I try my best to get along with everyone; I haven't gotten in a fist fight since the 9th grade, and he deserved it." Iris laughed silently against his chest. He was right – Peter Rhamos *did* deserve it. He was picking on Ivy, and Declan stood up against him, just like he always stood up to the bullies of the world. "No one knows what it's really like to be me."

She draped her arms around his neck, running her fingers through his hair as they cuddled close. "It's true," she said into the stillness. "You make it all seem easy. Even as close as we were, I didn't know. If I'd had any idea of what you were going through…"

"You would've pitied me, and 20-year-old me wouldn't have dealt well with that," Declan said bluntly. "Even 35-year-old me isn't liking the situation all that much."

She continued to stroke her fingers through his hair. "Dec, it isn't pity, like you'd feel for a homeless puppy dog," she said softly into his ear. "It's understanding. You make a lot more sense when parts of you aren't completely hidden from me."

"When have I ever confused you?" he protested.

She rolled her eyes, even as she kept her head snuggled up against him. "Ummmm…there was that time that you broke up with me for no reason whatsoever," she reminded him.

"Oh."

He didn't seem to have much else to say to that, but Iris couldn't stop. Not yet. "There was also that time you insisted that Miller boys are row crop farmers, not pig farmers, and were inexcusably rude to Mr. Harther in the process."

He didn't seem to have much to say to that either, and Iris decided to have pity on him and stop while she was ahead.

"Thank you for telling me," she whispered. "It means a lot that you trusted me enough to tell me the truth."

His arms were wrapped around her and he was stroking his hands through her hair, slowly, languidly, comfortingly. "I should've done it a long time ago. I know that now. We wasted a lot of time that we could've been—"

She pulled back and placed her index finger on his lips, stopping him. "Regrets won't fix any of this," she said, staring him straight in the eye. "We can't go back in time and fix anything. And you know what? I don't know if I'd want to, anyway. If it wasn't this, it probably would've been something else. We were just kids. I didn't know what I wanted, not really. I loved you…as much as a teenager can love anyone. But it's a lot deeper, and it means a lot more, now that we're adults. We can choose to be together, and we can keep making that choice, over and over again. For the rest of our lives."

"I think we ought to choose to be together right now," Declan said, his eyes hooded and dark with lust.

"I like how you think," Iris sighed, and then they reenacted the first time they made love, but this time, there was knowledge and passion and wisdom, along with lust.

She was right, of course. Everything was better now that they were adults.

EPILOGUE

IRIS

Early May, 2018

She looked around the Miller family barn, taking in its thick wooden rustic beams bedecked with strings of white lights and hay bales stacked in the corner. Considering that it was Stetson's barn, the irony was thick that he was the only one of the brothers who didn't get married in it. Jennifer didn't seem to mind, though.

"Helping other people plan their weddings is a lot more fun than planning your own," she said conspiratorially to Iris one day. "Especially if your mother likes to hover, like mine does, and especially if you're dealing with pregnancy hormones on top of everything else."

Iris' hands touched her flat stomach for a moment. If she was pregnant, she didn't know it. It wasn't for a lack of trying, though, that was for sure. She grinned to herself.

It was just a couple of hours until their wedding and reception would begin. It was crazy to think that it was in this barn, just a little over seven months ago, when she tried to hide from Declan behind Ms. Stout.

Getting caught staring at him was, hands down, the best thing that had ever happened to her. Other than maybe becoming his Spanish tutor. Or when he asked her out for the first time. Or when he asked her out for the second first time. That was pretty damn awesome.

No, really, when he finally told her the truth about his dyslexia and ended up proposing to her – that was the best thing that had ever happened to her.

All because of pigs. If she'd told her teenage self that someday, she'd be thrilled that the love of her life was brave enough to raise pigs, she probably would've laughed until she peed her pants. Being a pig farmer's wife hadn't exactly been the stuff of teenage daydreams. She'd watched a lot of Disney movies in her lifetime, and she had yet to run into that particular storyline.

But somehow, with Declan, it just felt right. Everything with Declan felt right.

"C'mon, Iris, you've got to go get ready," Ivy said at her elbow, tugging her out of her wandering thoughts. "You can't get married in that!"

Iris looked down at her beat-up Wranglers and dusty cowboy boots – her work attire she'd put on to help get the barn ready for their big night. She'd felt stable enough on her feet to actually help, although she was careful never to carry anything too terribly important…or breakable.

She let Ivy drag her towards Stetson's farmhouse so she could put on her wedding dress…and cowboy boots.

∼

THE DJ CALLED out to the gathering crowd, "The father of the bride has something he'd like to say, so y'all just quiet on down so he can talk."

A ripple of laughter ran through the crowd, but people obediently hushed. Iris cocked her head to the side, curious what her father was going to say. Her mom was the talker. Her dad didn't say much, even to his daughters.

Her dad took the mic and cleared his throat once, causing a feedback loop to erupt and shriek into everyone's eardrums. The crowd busted up laughing, and instead of growing more anxious because of the problem, her dad just grinned down at the crowd instead. "I wanted to make sure y'all were awake," he drawled.

Iris tucked herself in closer to Declan's side as she laughed along with the crowd. Had her dad had a few beers before he got up there to speak? Whatever was going on, it was fun to see.

Declan's hand ran up and down her right arm

and she snuggled in even closer with a happy sigh. Being there next to him…it was where she wanted to be.

Always and forever.

"As y'all have probably figured out by now, Declan is my new son-in-law." Her dad waited for the roar of the crowd to die down, and then continued, "Usually, a dad is sad to see his daughter marry and move on with her life, but in my case, all I can say is, 'It's about time.'"

The roar of laughter was even louder that time, and Iris turned her face into Declan's chest with embarrassment. It was true that their courtship of 20 years was a little on the long side.

Declan's chuckle reverberated through her. "Better late than never, right, sir?" he called out.

"Damn straight," her dad said, straight-faced, and then shot Declan a grin. "If it takes years for you to pull your head out of your ass, well, at least you did it!"

This time, Declan's laughter vibrated through his whole body, and Iris' laughter matched it.

"C'mon, Dad, I finally convinced him to do this!" she called out. "Don't go discouraging him now! He might change his mind!"

The crowd, in full laughter mode by this time, let out a howl at that. Declan pulled her up to his mouth and whispered, "Never," sending shivers down her spine. She grinned up at him and he kissed her on the nose, growling possessively at her.

Finally, her dad turned serious, pulling their attention back to him. "Declan, I want to welcome you to the family. Thanks for all you've done for my Iris. Treat her well."

"Yes, sir," Declan called back.

"Usually, the first dance is a daddy-daughter dance," her dad said, and sent her a misty-eyed glance. "But this time, I think Declan ought to have the honors." He turned and whispered something to the DJ, standing off to the side, and with a nod of the head, the DJ pressed play. Strains of *The Dance* by Garth Brooks filled the air, and Iris felt her eyes fill with tears.

Looking down at her, Declan murmured, "May I have this dance?"

She nodded once, and clung to his arm as they walked out onto the sawdust dance floor. She could trust Declan to hold her up. She knew that now.

The crowd around them faded to a blur as she looked into Declan's eyes. As they swayed together under the twinkle lights, he looked at her solemnly. "I will always hold you up," he whispered to her.

Her smile grew tremulous at that. Somehow, he'd unconsciously echoed her exact thoughts. "I know that now," she whispered back. Some part of her mind recognized the fact that other couples were moving out onto the dance floor, but none of that mattered now.

Nothing but Declan mattered now.

"Thank you for believing in me," he whispered.

"Thank you for trusting me. Thank you for loving me."

Her smile went from tremulous to downright tearful. "Always," she murmured, and buried her face against his chest. The haunting lyrics swirled around them as they moved to the music, and Iris knew that whatever happened, she could always trust Declan to be her rock, her guiding star…

Her love.

∾

Quick Author's Note

Damn, I sure love Declan and Iris' story! That ending brings tears to my eyes every time.

More than just being a touching story, though, it's actually based on a true story from one of my readers. (Hi, Yvette!)

So, a bit of backstory: I was chatting with Yvette via email before I even wrote *Returning for Love*, and that's when she shared with me that she had a brain injury that's affected her ability to move without falling over, along with causing other physical and emotional problems.

Her story made me tear up, and I knew as soon as I read it that this was the story I wanted to tell in *Returning*. Brain injuries are some of the hardest to deal with because it isn't always obvious from the outside that there's anything wrong. If someone has a broken leg, you know to step to the side and let them pass you. If someone has a broken brain, you might have no idea what's causing them to act the way that they are.

In fact, Yvette wrote a really touching poem about her disability, and with her permission, I'm including it here:

My Stroke
I don't look any different so you really can't tell,
I have a quick wit so I'm still funny as hell,
I lost 65% of my vision but I can still see,
My memory is a bit slow but I'm still me,
I stumble a lot but I can still walk,
My speech is a bit stilted but I can still talk,
My left side feels weird but I can still feel,
My body is in pain but I pray that it will heal,
I can't do a lot with my wonky left hand,
My right is half missing but I do the best that I can,
I think the hardest part of my disability,
Is with strangers it causes invisibility,
So please don't ignore me or pretend I'm not there,
I have so much to give and I'll share it, I swear.

— YVETTE NOLEN

Yvette, I hope I did your story justice. Thank you for being willing to share it with me. 🩶

Along with that side of the equation, I also wanted to show that Declan's brain was broken in its own way. After spending his whole life trying to hide this fact from the world, finally telling the truth to someone was a leap of faith that he could've only taken with Iris. It's a heartwarming example of love bringing out the best in you, and one of the reasons why I love romance stories so much. (I'm totally a romantic sap – I'll own it!)

Writing *Returning*, though, meant that I was also partially writing *Christmas of Love* at the same time (the next book in the Long Valley series). You'll see what I mean when you read *Christmas*, but basically, it's the same time period and some of the scenes are even the same, but they're all being told from Ivy or Austin's point of view, instead of Declan or Iris'.

There's a scene in *Christmas* that is ripped straight out of my own life, actually. I'm not going to tell you more than that and ruin it for you, but I will say that despite the fact that *Christmas of Love* is "only" a holiday novel, it packs quite a wallop.

Ivy has a story that needs to be told, and this is her chance…

~Erin

. . .

PS If *Returning for Love* happens to be the first book of mine that you've read, you should definitely start back on Book 1, *Accounting for Love*. It's the love story of Stetson and Jennifer, and is the introduction to the whole Long Valley world. So be sure to find it on your favorite storefront or local library.

But if you've already read the other books in the Long Valley series so far and are just anxious to get onto the next one, don't let me stand in your way!

Come, spend a Christmas in Long Valley, and fall in love along the way…

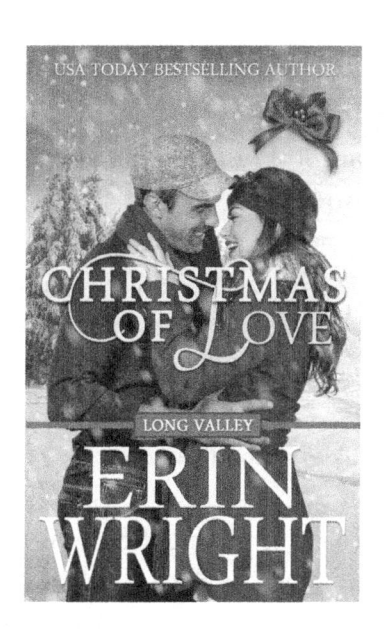

Christmas of Love

Next stop: Pain and heartache, coming right up...

Ivy McLain's grand scheme of making it big? Yeah, it's going nowhere fast. Every day, her dreams of a fabulous art career are fading a little more. And just when she didn't believe things could get any worse, her parents plan their huge 40th anniversary party.

In December.

In cold, snowy Podunk, Idaho.

It's been five years since Ivy's stepped foot in her hometown, and that was on purpose, thankyouverymuch. The oversized wide spot in the road holds nothing but truly awful memories for her.

All right, fine.

She's stuck having to return, and she's stuck playing the part of a dutiful daughter, but that doesn't mean she has to like it.

All of that changes the moment she meets a rugged cowboy with a slow and sexy smile.

Okay, bowls him over and spills his drink everywhere. Details, details…

Up next: A girl to tear your heart apart…

Austin Bishop is hiding from the world in the small, mountain town of Sawyer, Idaho.

Okay, maybe not from the world, but definitely from the *females* of the world.

It isn't that he thinks they have cooties. After all, he'd had a childhood sweetheart who he'd loved with all of his heart and soul for five years…right up until she dumped him. Receiving her engagement ring in the mail wasn't exactly the Christmas present he'd been hoping for that year.

That's all behind him, though. He is girl-free, and thrilled to be that way. Never better. Couldn't be happier, actually.

All the way up until he runs, quite literally, into the most beautiful, curvy redhead he's ever seen in his life. Suddenly, canoodling under the mistletoe seems like the best Christmas activity this side of eating homemade snickerdoodles. A fling with no strings attached? There's no better way to celebrate the holidays.

Except, partway through the twelve days of Christmas, it stops being a fling and starts feeling like a whole lot more.

But Ivy is hiding secrets, and so is he.

When their secrets unravel, can their relationship last? Or will their Christmas romance fizzle once the eggnog runs out?

∼

Read on for a taste of *Christmas*…

CHRISTMAS OF LOVE PREVIEW

IVY

December, 2017

Well, this party was exactly as exciting as Ivy McLain thought it was going to be.

Which was to say, not very exciting at all.

Of course, this was Sawyer, Idaho. What else could she expect?

She sighed. Only this, unfortunately. A bunch of old farmers, standing around and jawing about how their crops didn't bring in enough money and there wasn't enough water this past year, or maybe there was *too* much water, and the combine broke down in the field again…

It was enough to make Ivy's head hurt. Why people intentionally chose to live this way was beyond her. Especially the cold part. She shivered, pulling her woefully inadequate jacket tighter around herself. *Ugh.* A little over two weeks before Christmas in Sawyer freakin' Idaho. She should be grateful it wasn't snowing, but she couldn't find it in herself to be that saintly.

It was too cold to be grateful *or* saintly.

Her mom looked up from her discussion with Mrs. Frank about plans for next year's garden, and waved. Ivy smiled as cheerfully as she could – which was to say, not cheerfully at all – and huffed out a breath. If she didn't love her parents so much, she never would've made herself come back here. Thank God it was just a weekend visit. To actually *live* in Sawyer again…

Another shiver ran through her – from disgust or cold, she couldn't tell – and she spun on her heel to head towards the refreshment table. She'd make herself some hot cocoa and—

"Oof!" she gasped, when she ran into a brick wall.

She looked up to see…

Well, the cutest brick wall she'd ever laid eyes on. The phrase "tall, dark, and handsome" was definitely appropriate. Thick brown hair just long enough to run her fingers through, and the most piercing emerald green eyes she'd ever had the pleasure to see. Whiplash quick, he reached out a hand to steady her, gripping her elbow to keep her upright.

"Howdy," he said, pushing his cowboy hat a little further up on his head. In his hand was a mug of mulled apple cider.

An *empty* mug of mulled apple cider, because she'd spilled it all over him with her clumsiness.

The world froze as she realized what she'd done. Dammit all, she was a waitress! She knew how to navigate in tight spots. What on earth was she doing, running people over like that? A painful silence stretched between them, a chasm as she stared at the damage she'd wreaked.

And then the dam broke, and the words came tumbling out.

"So sorry!" she gasped, looking at his jacket, covered in a brown liquid that was now dripping off onto the frozen ground. "So, so sorry. I wasn't watching where I was going and then you were there and…let me help clean you up. It's the least I can do." Not waiting for his response, she began dragging him towards the refreshment table, thankfully only a few feet away. She'd get him cleaned up and on his way, and then she'd run and hide in her parent's broom closet.

Preferably for the next year or so.

"No worries!" he said with a low chuckle as he hurried along behind her. She stopped abruptly at the table and began grabbing the paper towels. "This jacket needs to be dry cleaned anyway," he continued. "Kept meaning to take it on over to the Wash 'N Spin, but haven't had—"

Which is when she started patting his face dry, and he had to shut up. *Dammit, dammit, dammit.* She'd gotten apple cider everywhere. How on earth did she get it on his earlobe?! She was patting him dry and trying really hard to ignore his strong jaw covered with a light dusting of dark brown hair and green eyes and—

Just get this done already, Ivy!

Her pats were coming a little slower, though, as she got caught up in his gaze. They were only inches apart from each other, and sure, her hands were filled with dirty paper towels, and sure, his jacket was sticky to the touch from the cider, but in that moment?

None of that mattered.

All she could do was stare at him. She caught her lower lip between her teeth, her breath uneven.

"My name is Austin Bishop," he said, breaking the silence between them. "And yours is?"

Right. Name.

She probably should've thought to introduce herself before she put her hands all over his body, but better late than never, right?

"Ivy McLain," she said, proud that she could get her name out at all. She sounded breathless, but she *was* breathless, so there wasn't much to be done about that.

"I thought you looked like Iris," he said, with what was possibly the cutest grin she'd ever seen on a man's face.

"People say I look like her," Ivy said with a shrug, happy to note that her voice didn't sound quite as breathless as it had before. "I don't see it, personally."

"You don't see..." His voice trailed off and he cocked an eyebrow at her in disbelief. "You two could be twins," he said bluntly.

Ivy threw her head back and laughed. It was sweet of him to say, of course. And she wasn't going to be coy and demure and say that it wasn't true – even though it really wasn't – in an attempt to get him to give her more compliments.

But everyone knew that Iris was the prettier of the two, and there was no use pretending otherwise.

"So why the plant names?" Austin asked after her chuckles had died down a bit. His gaze was as intense as ever, like he was trying to memorize every curve, every freckle, every laugh wrinkle on her face. It was disconcerting to have someone look at her so…intently.

She tried not to read too much into it, though. He probably looked at everyone that way.

She shrugged. "My parents wanted us girls to remember 'our roots,' so they named us after plants. Mostly what ended up happening was they couldn't keep our names straight. I kid you not – I thought my name was Iris-Ivy for the longest time."

He chuckled, and a warmth spread through her that belied the brisk winter temperatures. She wanted to lean into him again, but this time, not be blotting up spilled apple cider. She wanted—

"Oh, there you are!"

The voice cut through the cold air like a whip – slicing through Ivy's heart and sending spasms of pain through her. *No, not her. She can't be here! Iris promised me she wouldn't invite—*

And then Tiffany was draping herself over Austin,

practically climbing up his side. Tiffany sent Ivy a sickeningly sweet smile that didn't even vaguely reach her eyes, as she looked her up and down. Dismissing her, Tiffany turned back to Austin. "I didn't realize you'd be here, darlin'," she cooed. "I tried calling you about going to the ice skating show tomorrow night, but you didn't answer." She ran her fingers up his chest and to his face, bopping him on the nose playfully. If she was going to get any closer to him, she'd have to strip naked to do it.

Ivy began backing up, mumbling something that could've been, "Have a good time," or "Good food tonight," or "I hope you eat bugs and die…"

Really, it was quite mumbled, and even she wasn't sure what she said, and then she was spinning on her heel and heading towards the house, the dirtied paper towels still in her hands. She began wringing them in her hands as she walked.

"Austin and Tiffany?" she muttered under her breath as she stalked, blinded by rage as she went. "Tiffany?!" She could forgive him for anyone but Tiffany.

Okay, maybe not Ezzy, either.

But anyone but Tiffany or Ezzy, she could understand. But those two…they just didn't seem his type.

Not that she knew his type. She barely knew his name. But floozy, bitchy girls didn't seem like they should be anyone's type, if you asked her.

Not that anyone had, of course.

She tossed the dirty paper towels into a trashcan as she passed, and then stormed into the kitchen, muttering as she went. "Damn Tiffany, always ruining – Iris!" she yelped in surprise when she spotted her sister at the sink. Beautiful as ever, but a little more fragile than she used to be, Iris turned and shot her a smile.

Ivy scowled. Her sister had promised not to invite those two to the party. "You would not believe who is here!" she announced as she headed for the fruit platter on the counter. Yum – honeycrisp apples. They were her fav, and really only available in the fall and early winter. Which made them an even bigger treat when she could get her hands on them. She snatched one up and began crunching on it as she paced her parent's small kitchen.

Iris grabbed another potato and gave it a light scrub. "Yeah?" she prompted. She looked like she was in the middle of making the infamous McLain potato salad, which was awesome. If Ivy was going to be stuck in Long Valley for a weekend, she might as well enjoy something amazing to eat.

"Tiffany and Ezzy! You didn't invite them, did you?" Ivy asked around a mouthful of apple.

Iris turned, and without a word, sent Ivy a death glare.

That death glare. The patented Iris Blue McLain death glare.

Ever since they were kids, Iris had been able to kill

with just a look, a look that always made Ivy feel about three feet tall.

Turns out, Iris hadn't lost her touch when it came to her glares.

Ivy shrunk back. "I didn't think so, I just thought I'd ask," she mumbled sheepishly.

Iris just continued to glare, and Ivy continued to feel awful. On second thought, that was a really terrible thing to accuse her sister of doing. Iris knew just as well as anyone how miserable Tiffany and Ezzy had made her life all the way through school. She never would've invited them here on purpose.

Ivy knew that…when she wasn't wrapped up in her own little anger-induced pity party.

When the silence extended out into painful territory, finally Ivy mumbled, "I'm sorry. I shouldn't have said that."

Iris nodded her head – just once, regally, like a queen forgiving her subjects – and just like that, things were okay again. Iris began gathering the potatoes from the kitchen sink and moving them over to the table.

She probably needed to sit down. Ever since her car wreck three months ago, Iris had struggled with simple things, like standing. Or walking. Or staying upright.

It was painful for Ivy to see. Her sister had been the basketball star of Long Valley. She'd helped Sawyer win state championships. She was captain of the girl's basketball team as both a junior *and* a senior.

She had more athletic talent in her little pinky toe than Ivy did in her whole body, something the whole valley now knew.

When the high school coach had first welcomed Ivy onto the basketball court, his eyes had been bright with excitement. He'd been handed a gift – another McLain who'd help extend the Sawyer High School winning streak for another three years after Iris had graduated and moved on to college.

It was an excitement that quickly fizzled out when he saw Ivy's ball handling skills, which were...nonexistent.

She'd ended up on the JV team all four years of high school.

That sort of thing just wasn't what a soul could live down in a small town.

Ivy snapped her head up as Iris began to muse, "My best guess is that they heard about the free food and music, and decided to come on down and mooch off us. They're the kinds of people who would think that'd be okay."

Ivy considered that for a moment and then sighed. "You're right." She grabbed the last item – a bowl of washed potatoes – and carried them over to the table for Iris. She should've been paying attention instead of wallowing in her own insecurities, and helped Iris with more of the items. Iris smiled up at her with gratitude anyway, and Ivy forced herself to smile back.

Some days, Iris could be infuriatingly kind. It

really wasn't fair that she was *that* pretty and *that* talented and *that* nice.

"Thanks, sis," Iris said cheerfully, oblivious to Ivy's inner turmoil, and drew the bowl towards her, pulling out potatoes so she could begin chopping them.

Ivy headed back to the fruit platter on the counter. Those honeycrisp apples were some of the best she'd ever had, and she couldn't seem to keep her hands off them.

"Well, they've ruined everything," she informed Iris around a mouthful of apple.

"Everything?" Iris echoed skeptically.

"Yeah! There was this guy, and—"

"Hey, you guys, I need to know where you want this table," one of the caterers said, popping his head around the kitchen door.

Iris started to struggle to her feet, but Ivy waved her off. "You sit and take a break and get the damn salad done already. There are rumblings in the ranks that no one has brought the famous McLain salad out yet. I'll go." It was about time she helped out, instead of just mooning over cowboys. She snagged another apple slice and headed out the door, listening as the caterer outlined the issue. She would get this straightened out, and *then* go hide in her parent's broom closet. It was the least she could do for Iris, and for her parents.

It wasn't their fault that returning to Long Valley was the disaster she knew it would be. That blame could be laid squarely at the feet of two women who'd spent years of their lives making Ivy's life miserable...

And one hunky cowboy with *terrible* taste in women.

She was flying back to California tomorrow, and already, she couldn't wait.

∽

Available at your favorite retailer or library – pick your copy up today!

ALSO BY ERIN WRIGHT

~ LONG VALLEY ~

Accounting for Love

Blizzard of Love

Arrested by Love

Returning for Love

Christmas of Love

Overdue for Love

Bundle of Love

Lessons in Love

Baked with Love

Bloom of Love (2021)

Holly and Love (TBA)

Banking on Love (TBA)

Sheltered by Love (TBA)

Conflicted by Love (TBA)

~ FIREFIGHTERS OF LONG VALLEY ~

Flames of Love

Inferno of Love

Fire and Love

Burned by Love

~ MUSICIANS OF LONG VALLEY ~

Strummin' Up Love

Melody of Love (TBA)

Rock 'N Love (TBA)

Rhapsody of Love (TBA)

~ SERVICEMEN OF LONG VALLEY ~

Thankful for Love (2021)

Commanded to Love (TBA)

Salute to Love (TBA)

Harbored by Love (TBA)

ABOUT ERIN WRIGHT

USA Today Bestselling author Erin Wright has worked every job under the sun, including library director, barista, teacher, website designer, and ranch hand helping brand cattle, before settling into the career she's always dreamed about: Author.

She still loves coffee, doesn't love the smell of cow flesh burning, and has embarked on the adventure of a lifetime, traveling the country full-time in an RV. (No one has died yet in the confined 250-square-foot space – which she considers a real win – but let's be real, next week isn't looking so good…)

Find her updates on ErinWright.net, where you can sign up for her newsletter along with the requisite pictures of Jasmine the Writing Cat, her kitty cat muse and snuggle buddy extraordinaire.

Wanna get in touch?
www.erinwright.net
erin@erinwright.net

Or reach out to Erin on your favorite social media platform:

- facebook.com/AuthorErinWright
- twitter.com/erinwrightlv
- pinterest.com/erinwrightbooks
- goodreads.com/erinwright
- bookbub.com/profile/erin-wright
- instagram.com/authorerinwright

Made in the USA
Monee, IL
09 February 2024